u

by

u

2

La detective
está muerta.

The Detective Is Already Dead

"Oh, uh. Well...... It looks good on you."

When the curtain finally opened, there was Siesta in a pure-white wedding dress.

"How is it?"

"I thought I'd make an apple pie. You'd said you were going to the trouble of buying some apples, so..."

Siesta's hands moved cheerfully.

"Heh-heh! I mean, you know, you seem to have taken quite a liking to me, after all. I suppose this is my way of taking responsibility for being the object of someone's affections; I thought I could do this much for you, at least."

Proxy Detective
(Little Girl)

Alicia

A young girl with amnesia whom Kimizuka brought home. Siesta makes her a proxy detective.

Siesta was wearing a bathrobe, just like I was, and every time she bounced, certain *other* parts bounced dramatically, too. ...Or maybe they only seemed to because my head wasn't really working, either.

"And so theeen, I was still little, so I got really nervous when I swallowed the watermelon seed. I thought it might sprout in my stomach, and *then* what would I do?"

Occupation	**Student**
Grade	**Middle school, second year**
Favorite Subject	**Music**
Committee	**Library Committee member**
Club	**Mystery Research Club president**
Likes	**Napping, teasing the vice president**
Code	**Be skilled in both pen and sword**

Her beautiful blue eyes weren't even remotely Japanese. Her cool expression radiated an indescribable charm that reminded me of the transition from girlhood to maturity. The red ribbon in her pale-silver hair bloomed like a lone flower, and in that uniform—from the crown of her head to the tips of her toes, she was as beautiful as a flawless sculpture.

(Excerpt from the memoirs of the vice president)

The Detective Is Already Dead

2

nigozyu

Illustration by Umibouzu

YEN ON

New York

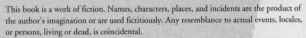

The Detective Is Already Dead, Vol. 2

nigozyu

Translation by Taylor Engel
Cover art by Umibouzu

TANTEI HA MO, SHINDEIRU. Vol.2
©nigozyu 2020
First published in Japan in 2020 by KADOKAWA CORPORATION, Tokyo.
English translation rights arranged with KADOKAWA CORPORATION, Tokyo,
through TUTTLE-MORI AGENCY, INC., Tokyo.

Yen On
150 West 30th Street, 19th Floor
New York, NY 10001

Visit us at yenpress.com
facebook.com/yenpress
twitter.com/yenpress
yenpress.tumblr.com
instagram.com/yenpress

First Yen On Edition: November 2021

Yen On is an imprint of Yen Press, LLC.
The Yen On name and logo are trademarks of Yen Press, LLC.

The publisher is not responsible for websites (or their content) that are not owned by the publisher.

Library of Congress Cataloging-in-Publication Data
Names: nigozyu, author. | Umibouzu, illustrator. | Engel, Taylor, translator.
Title: The detective is already dead / nigozyu ; illustration by Umibouzu ;
    translation by Taylor Engel.
Other titles: Tantei wa Mou, Shindeiru. English
Description: First Yen On edition. | New York, NY : Yen On, 2021.
Identifiers: LCCN 2021012132 | ISBN 9781975325756 (v. 1 ; trade paperback);
    ISBN 9781975325770 (v. 2 ; trade paperback)
Subjects: GSAFD: Mystery fiction.
Classification: LCC PL873.5.I46 T3613 2021 | DDC 895.63/6—dc23
LC record available at https://lccn.loc.gov/2021012132

ISBNs: 978-1-9753-2577-0 (paperback)
       978-1-9753-2578-7 (ebook)

10 9 8 7 6 5 4 3 2 1

LSC-C

Printed in the United States of America

The DetECtiVe Is AlreadY Dead

2

Contents

Prologue

I was dreaming.

It was a long, fantastical dream, almost like a fairy tale.

Ten thousand meters above the earth, I met a girl, and for the next three years, we went on an unforgettable series of adventures.

In Singapore, we gambled at casinos and played on the beaches and searched for a legendary hidden treasure.

In New York, we were watching a musical until terrorists got involved.

In Venice, the City of Water, we pursued a notorious phantom thief who was trying to make a getaway in a dramatic boat chase through the canals.

We trekked across deserts, forged through jungles, crossed mountains, sailed over oceans—journeyed all over the world.

Finally, in London, we encountered a diabolical villain, whose secret base proved to be our final destination.

The girl who was my partner confronted the villain.

I was watching the scene play out from behind her, but all of a sudden my vision went blurry, and my hearing started to fade.

I quickly tried to shout, but I couldn't make a sound.

This has to be a dream. Just a horrific nightmare.

I knew it logically, and yet I couldn't shake the fear.

As I struggled with my thoughts, the enemy raised a huge blade. It was going to strike my partner unless someone intervened.

I screamed her name, or tried to, but my voice still wasn't working.

As despair welled up within me—my partner turned halfway back toward me.

She was saying something. Telling me something.

…But I couldn't hear her voice.

Desperately, I tried to read her lips, but my vision was fading.

A moment later, blood dyed the girl's face.

She was dead.

However...I'd been able to make out one thing. Just one.

Right before she died, my partner had looked at me with a lonely smile.

That was the sort of dream I was having.

"You're the ace detective?"

That ridiculous question was what pulled me out of my dream.

The classroom was empty, and the sun was going down outside.

I must have dozed off at some point, and someone had been kind enough to wake me. Rubbing my bleary eyes, I raised my head.

It was a girl in my grade, but I didn't recognize her.

Then, for some unfathomable reason, she hauled me up by the shirt-front and started threatening me in ways I didn't really understand. My knack for getting dragged into trouble hadn't gotten any better.

"Oh, I see. Yes, of course: *You wanted me to hold you close, didn't you?*"

That wasn't a thought I was having, but she pressed me to her chest anyway.

The marshmallowy softness and the sweet scent of her perfume threatened to dissolve my brain.

I could also hear *her heart.*

Badmp, badmp.

Badmp, badmp.

The sound was so familiar. Why was that?

Thinking it was odd, I asked the girl her name.

And she told me it was—

"......Hmm?"

A sweet scent and a springy sensation against my cheek woke me.

Ah—*waking up was part of the dream, too.*

The room was dark, and I couldn't make out much. But the scent and the softness from the dream were definitely there. So what was this?

"Waaaaaaaaaaaaaaaaaaaaaaaaagh!"

There was a scream, and a sharp pain ran through my cheek. Not fair…

"—! What the heck was that for, Natsunagi?"

I glared at the girl, the one I assumed had just slapped me.

"What the heck were *you* doing?! Don't just grope your classmate's chest the second you wake up! Have some shame!"

"The first time we met, I'm pretty sure you forced me to feel up your chest."

"—! I already told you, I wasn't exactly myself when I did that!"

The girl who was yelling was Nagisa Natsunagi. She was in my grade in high school, and she was an ace detective.

We'd gotten to know each other when I'd taken a certain job. Then we got involved in a couple more cases, and along the way, she'd become the detective, I'd become her assistant, and we'd developed a sort of friend-ship that neither of us seemed able to shake. That said, I didn't remember sleeping together being part of the arrangement…

"So, where is this?" Natsunagi twisted around curiously. We were lying on a cold concrete floor. She didn't recognize this place any better than I did.

"…Yeah, where *are* we?"

I dredged my memory, which I should have done earlier. Why had Nat-sunagi been lying beside me when I woke up? What time was it, and what was this place? What had I been doing yesterday…?

"Uhnn… Would you two quiet down already?"

I felt something land on my knee with a light *thunk*.

"That voice… Saikawa?"

I didn't recall making any indication that she had permission to use my lap as a pillow… That aside, it definitely was her voice.

Yui Saikawa was Japan's top idol, and the first client Natsunagi and I had picked up. Ever since we'd solved her case, we'd been close enough to banter back and forth… But…

"Saikawa, why are you here, too?"

"Huh? Why am I sleeping with you, you mean? You're asking *me* that?"

"What's with the suggestive phrasing? …Wait, I didn't bring you in here, did I?"

"Hang on a second, is that what's going on?" Natsunagi cried. "You brought Yui in here, and you pushed me down onto the hard floor, and tied me up, and then—!"

"Natsunagi, your fantasies might be affecting your memory. You're not tied up, all right?"

This was a disaster—I was starting to think figuring out where we'd found ourselves would be more trouble than it was worth. But then:

"If you're going to play games, do you suppose you could save it for later, Kimizuka?"

The voice was cold and cross, and the harshness toward me specifically told me instantly who she was.

"So you're here, too, huh, Charlie?"

Charlotte Arisaka Anderson. She was another old connection I couldn't seem to get rid of: a girl about my age with whom I'd worked frequently. After another recent case, we'd gradually made peace with each other... but clearly, she hadn't softened her attitude toward me.

"You people seriously don't remember? We were on our way to visit Ma'am's grave when *somebody kidnapped us and brought us here.*"

"...!"

Oh, right. I remembered now. Yesterday, the four of us had been on our way to visit my former partner's grave.

It had started a few days earlier, when the cruise Saikawa was hosting had gotten seajacked. After we'd defeated the pseudohuman Chameleon, Charlie and I had reconciled by mutually taking up Siesta's last wish, then promised to visit her grave.

Of course, that would have been an extremely awkward trip with just the two of us, so yesterday Natsunagi and Saikawa had joined us on the visit to her grave... But on the way, someone had attacked us and brought us here.

"I swear, you people are always so careless," Charlie sniffed, crossing her arms arrogantly (it was too dark to actually see her, but I'd bet you anything she did).

"Uh, except you got kidnapped, too."

"You've also been kidnapped, Charlie."

"Weren't you kidnapped as well, Charlie?"

"...! Argh, fine, I'm sorry!" Charlie's shrill voice echoed in the dark room.

We weren't acting nearly as worried as we should have been. *Our captor's probably wishing they hadn't wasted their time kidnapping us right about now*, I thought with a chagrined smirk—

"Ahh...!" Natsunagi held up a hand to shield her face from the sudden light.

A screen at the front of the room had come on.

"Dark cells and mysterious TV screens, hmm?"

Several "death game"–type scenarios raced across my mind. For example, in a moment the kidnapper would appear on that screen, wearing a mask, and lay out a set of fiendish rules.

"Ghk! First they bound us hand and foot, and now what? What on earth will they...?"

"Natsunagi, are you blushing?" I asked.

"If I recall, Kimizuka, weren't you planning to attend your little sister's wedding once this battle was over?" Saikawa asked.

"Don't try to jinx me to give yourself a better chance of survival," I snapped back at her.

"It's all right, Kimizuka," Charlie said. "No matter what type of death game this is, with my brains, we'll have no trouble."

"Lucky us!" I crowed. "Charlie just out-jinxed everybody."

"I wasn't trying to be funny!"

Come on, people, at least show a little fear. The poor kidnapper's not gonna know how to make a grand entrance after this.

Sheesh. Well, no matter what happens next or who shows up on that screen, I'm definitely not going to be too taken aback, I thought. That's what we were all thinking.

Which is why in the next instant...

When we saw the individual who did appear on the screen, we couldn't say anything.

"If this footage is playing, it means that Kimihiko Kimizuka, Nagisa Natsunagi, Yui Saikawa, and Charlotte Arisaka Anderson are all present."

It had been a year since I'd heard that voice—cool as a cucumber and yet so warm.

"Sies—"

"Ma'am!"

"Gweh."

I felt a sudden weight as Charlie climbed right onto my back for a better view of the screen.

The girl on the display had pale silver hair and blue eyes. It was my former partner, the deceased ace detective. Siesta.

Charlie had been her apprentice at one point, and she wasn't able to conceal her excitement at seeing Siesta again after a year apart. However...

"Charlie, this is a recording."

"Huh?!"

We couldn't let fleeting emotions trick us. Always stay calm and clever. There was no way Siesta could be here now. The detective was already dead.

"It's been a long time, Charlie, but I'm sorry. This is just a video; I recorded it a year ago, in anticipation of today."

As if Siesta had seen even this little exchange coming, she smiled softly at Charlie.

"Ma'am..." Charlie gazed sorrowfully through the screen at Siesta.

"I'm sorry to ask when things are getting emotional, but please get off me before you have this conversation."

Once again, the four of us turned toward the TV.

"So she's...," Natsunagi whispered.

"That's Siesta, then...," Saikawa said.

This was probably the first time either of them had actually seen her.

"Now then, there is a reason I've gathered you here," Siesta said, again as if she'd known exactly when the lull would be. "I think it's about time you knew...about what happened to me, one year ago."

One year ago—was the detective talking about the day she had died? The day she'd been killed by Chameleon?

"Chameleon didn't kill me."

Once again, Siesta seemed to have read my mind.

"No, but he said—"

I was sure Chameleon had said he'd killed her. Charlie sent a confused glance my way. She'd heard the same information straight from Chameleon as well, back during the battle on the ship.

"Assistant, I want you to remember." Siesta gazed at me.

"There's something you want me to remember?" I was forgetting something? Forgetting what?

"I'd also like the rest of you to know. Once you do—I want you to *decide*."

In the next moment, the screen cut to a different image. It was the interior of the airplane where I'd met Siesta four years ago, at ten thousand meters.

"What's...?"

"It's a record of all I've seen up to this point. The three years I spent with you."

...! It couldn't be. Was she planning to tell us about that record, those memories, right now? Was this supposed to help me remember whatever she needed me to?

"All right, are you ready? We'll start four years ago."

No sooner had Siesta appeared on the monitor again than she told us:

"I want you to watch this to the end. You'll see what happened to us. The truth of my death. And my last fight—"

Chapter 1

◆ Nothing beats a (mixed) bath after a hijacking

"No way. I don't want to be your assistant."

In the bathroom of my run-down apartment, I squeezed my eyes shut to keep the shampoo out of them and once again vetoed the screwball proposal that had been pitched to me multiple times now.

"Huh? What? I couldn't hear you."

However, this particular pitcher didn't seem the least bit disturbed by my criticism. I suspected she wouldn't give up until I said yes.

"Yes, you definitely can," I complained to the person on the other side of the door, raising my volume a couple notches. My low voice bounced off the walls of the small room into a multilayered echo.

"Now, now, calm down. You're supposed to relax in the bath, you know."

"Yes, and I can't, thanks to *somebody*." I finished rinsing off the shampoo, then got into the cramped bathtub.

"Shall I wash your back for you?"

"No thanks."

"Maybe I'll walk in there wearing nothing but a towel."

"...No thanks."

"Certainly took you a moment, though."

Dammit, what kind of dastardly trap was she setting for a teenage guy? Actually, more importantly...

"Why are you in my apartment—Siesta?" I asked the girl standing in the dressing room.

Her code name was Siesta—a girl of indeterminate nationality, with pale silver hair and blue eyes.

Just a week ago, I'd met her on a passenger jet at ten thousand meters. She'd called herself an "ace detective," and the two of us had resolved a certain incident together. But for me, the incident hadn't ended there...

"Listen, Siesta, you can't just walk into people's houses uninvited. And don't try to get into the bathroom."

"Well, you aren't listening to what I have to say."

There it was again.

Immediately after the hijacking was over and done with, she'd started making ridiculous demands: "I want you to fly around the world with me as my assistant." I had no idea what was going through her mind.

Of course, the proposal was absolute nonsense, and I'd turned her down. However, Siesta showed no sign of folding. We'd been at it for a week now.

"You're awfully stubborn. Breaking in was no walk in the park, all right?"

"The hell? Why do you sound so proud of that? Am I the bad guy here?"

"I am the hero, after all. Going against me automatically makes you the bad guy."

What hero would use that ridiculous logic?

"Actually, I distinctly remember locking the door, so...?"

"Oh, that. I opened it with my master key. It's one of my Seven Tools; there's no lock this key can't open."

"Wow, almost sounds like it *was* a walk in the park."

"Hmm, that's rather annoying."

"Not as annoying as invading my privacy." Seriously, I thought I was gonna have a heart attack when I heard her voice through my bathroom door out of nowhere.

"So, we'd decided that I was going to wash your back, correct?"

"Look, quit trying to get in the bath with me at every opportunity." We'd only met a week ago, and she was already in my face. The future was looking bleak indeed...

"And? Why are you so against being my assistant?" Once again, Siesta asked me that question through the thin door. Good grief, she still wasn't giving up.

"'Cause I wanna be normal." In the narrow bathtub, I splashed hot water over my face. "I told you earlier, remember? I get dragged into stuff.

It's never brought me anything but trouble. All I want is to live in peace. Like a nice, tepid bath that won't burn me."

"And you're saying you won't be able to live that life if you're with me?"

"Well, not after you showed me *a thing like that.*"

I was thinking about the fight with the pseudohuman that had broken out at ten thousand meters.

A plain old hijacking wouldn't have been so bad. I mean, it certainly wouldn't have been *good,* but after what I'd seen, I wasn't gonna complain. But that *thing* was out of the question. If I got involved with whatever the hell that was, I wouldn't survive it no matter how many lives I had.

"But I'm the only one who can do this job," Siesta snapped. It was sharper than I'd ever heard her speak.

"Is there any point in dragging me into something only you can do?"

"Well... Oh, that's right."

"You're literally making something up as we speak, aren't you?"

"The truth is, I fell in love with you at first sight, and—"

"Except the one time we actually agreed to meet up, you didn't recognize me, remember?"

"Your face is so bland that I forget it if I don't see you for a couple of days. It's perfect for undercover operations."

"Enough with the backhanded compliments. And don't give me jobs when I haven't even agreed to assist you yet."

"...You really won't be my assistant?" Siesta's voice suddenly lowered.

Yeah. That's what I've been telling you this whole time. Why do you sound kinda depressed about it?

I swear. This was barely even a conversation, not that any of her attempts before were much better. It's all because Siesta won't say what she's actually thinking. She tries to get her way without offering anything to persuade me, so these discussions always come to nothing.

Even that hijacking. It had technically been resolved at one point, and yet Siesta had used her overwhelming fighting skills and dynamism to force the hijacker into submission. If that was how things were going to be, I saw no future in this.

"If you're trying to negotiate, start by telling me what's in it for me," I said, handing her commonsense advice instead.

...Don't get the wrong idea, though. I only did it so I could turn her down after we'd done the negotiations right. I didn't want this to drag on and on.

"Heh-heh! You're nicer than I thought, Kimi."

"You're overestimating me, then. Don't read between the lines."

"Come to think of it, I ordered a pizza a few minutes back; was that all right?"

"Don't immediately take advantage of people's kindness! Call in and cancel that right now!"

"This is just a conjecture, but I get the feeling that a year from now, we'll probably be getting along just fine like this."

"What about this is 'getting along just fine'?! What about me? I've been stressed out this whole time!"

I'm exhausted. Seriously, dealing with Siesta wears me out… It's just as I thought: There is nothing she could offer me that would convince me to be her assistant.

"Well?" she said. "Go on and talk."

"No, I didn't mean me. You were going to tell me what was in this for me, remember?"

However, as always, Siesta was acting as though she'd seen through everything. "You've got something worrying you, don't you?" she asked, through the door. "I can clear that up for you. That's a service I can provide."

"You're telling me to become your assistant, and in exchange, you'll solve my problem?"

"I may have said that, yes."

If I asked Siesta how she knew I was worrying about something, she probably wouldn't tell me. She was an ace detective who was only interested in results.

"…The thing is, there's some trouble at my middle school right now."

And so, after I got out of the bathtub, I said:

"Apparently they've had *a mass outbreak of Miss Hanakos of the Toilet.*"

As I dried myself off with a towel, I told the detective about that weird school mystery.

"I see. Sounds like I'll need to listen to that story carefully, over pizza."

"…Yeah. You can have pizza, so hurry up and shut that door again."

◆ Pizza, soda, foreign TV shows, and occasionally Miss Hanako of the Toilet

Miss Hanako of the Toilet is one of those "seven school wonders" that everyone's heard about at least once.

It goes like this: If you go into the girls' bathroom on the third floor of the old school building at three in the morning and knock three times on the door of the third stall in, a girl in a red jumper skirt will appear and drag you into the toilet...or something to that effect. It's the kind of outdated, garden-variety urban legend that wouldn't normally even be worth talking about. However—

"You're saying things are a little different at your school?" Siesta asked over her shoulder.

When I got out of the bathroom, Siesta was stuffing her face with pizza in the cramped, traditional, nine-square-meter tatami living room, her eyes on the foreign drama that was playing on the little TV. At some point after breaking into my home, she'd changed into the T-shirt I usually wore around the house and shifted completely into relaxation mode.

"So you barge into the apartment of a guy you've just met, borrow his clothes, and watch foreign dramas while you eat pizza. What are you, my live-in girlfriend?"

"Huh? Uh, no?"

"I know you're not. That's why I'm complaining." With the towel still draped over my head, I sat down near Siesta and reached for the pizza.

"Oh, the cheese half is mine, so don't eat any of it."

"You're the one who ordered it! How is that fair?"

"You can have the double-pickle kind."

"Don't make me dispose of your leftovers. Also, apologize to every pickle fan in the country."

"I really appreciate the fact that you're still eating it as you say that. You should continue to develop that trait."

"What do you mean, 'continue to develop it'? Why are you trying to mentor me? Who do you think you are?"

This was no good; the conversation was going nowhere. What had we been talking about, anyway?

"Hanako, right?"

"Oh yeah… But it's *Miss* Hanako. She's not your friend."

"And? You're saying this Miss Hanako is multiplying at your middle school?" Siesta reached for another piece of pizza.

"Yeah. From what I hear, at my school, students who run into Miss Hanako *end up becoming Miss Hanakos themselves.*"

"Ah. Like the way people who get bitten by zombies turn into zombies."

"Exactly. It's a rumor straight out of a B movie."

"Except it isn't just a rumor, and that's why you're telling me about it. Right?"

…Well, yes, that's about the size of it. Although I don't particularly want to admit it.

"Right now, a bunch of students have suddenly stopped coming to school, mainly from the track team, and the number's growing. The teachers won't give us any details…but I hear some of them have actually run away, instead of just skipping school."

One kid in my class had started staying home, and I knew of at least twenty or so more as a whole. Several of those were runaways, so the police were already involved.

"Has the track club had any internal trouble?"

"No idea. There haven't been any rumors of a falling out."

"I see… It may be an external factor, then. The sort of thing that would have a big, chain-reaction effect on an entire group." Her expression grave, Siesta chewed her pizza, then swallowed. "But you're saying the rumor at your school is that Miss Hanako may have dragged all the missing students into the girls' toilet?"

"Yeah. And since the number of missing kids is growing faster and faster, they're wondering whether the number of Miss Hanakos is growing, too."

That was why the mind-numbing rumor about a "mass outbreak of Miss Hanakos" was spreading through the school.

"Do you believe it, too, Kimi?"

"Hell no." I snorted, washing down my pickle-covered pizza with cola.

"Aw, look at you pretending to be omnipotent. Classic middle schooler."

"Don't come for me like this." I got the feeling I'd never beat this detective in an argument as long as I lived.

"...Still, they've stopped coming to school and gone missing, hmm?" Siesta said abruptly, her eyes still on the TV.

The program was an overseas drama set in an academy. In the current scene, there was a kid who'd stopped coming to class, and all of his class-mates had gone to his house to pick him up. Wouldn't that make him want to come to school even less...?

"You're a nice person, aren't you?" Siesta turned to look at me.

"You're still helping me pay for the pizza, all right?"

"That's not what I meant," she replied, then added, "And no, I'm not." *No, seriously. You need to pay me back.*

"Naturally, the students who disappeared from school aren't your friends, are they? And yet you're worried about them enough to want to resolve the problem."

"'Naturally'? What makes you so sure I don't have friends?"

"Maybe it's because of that tendency to get dragged into things you mentioned. At the same time, saving people seems to be part of your DNA, too."

...Yet another type of DNA I don't need. Well, anyway.

"I like keeping my immediate surroundings peaceful and normal, you know? I mean, this is what my life is usually like," I said, smiling wryly as I looked around the apartment. "By the time I was old enough to notice, my parents had evaporated. I bounced around between different houses and care facilities for a while, and now, I'm living on my own at fourteen. That'll make you want a peaceful, average, stable environment."

Well, as long as I had this curse, I knew it wasn't going to be easy. Still, trying to resolve as many problems as I was capable of handling on my own in my quest for a mediocre, commonplace routine couldn't possibly be a crime.

"I see, so that's your—" Siesta put a fingertip to her chin, as if she was thinking hard about something. "Mm-hmm. I understand everything."

"But we've barely talked. That's kinda freaky."

"Yes, I see. You must be pretty lonely without any family or friends."

"Look, did I ever say I didn't have friends? Could you stop making random guesses?"

But she was right that I didn't have many. I also couldn't remember the last time I'd talked with a classmate. Still.

"All right. This weekend, let's go to that together."

Siesta was pointing at the TV. On the screen, a girl who seemed to be the heroine was taking the truant boy to a school festival.

"...Uh, what happened to the Miss Hanako thing?"

◆ And now for the teen rom-com shenanigans

"I'm still kinda expecting this to turn into a mystery-horror story, all right?"

Avoiding the weird middle schooler muttering to himself, students and visitors streamed through the school gate.

It was some days later, a Saturday, and I was waiting for someone at the gate of my middle school. Even though it was a weekend morning, the gate was quite busy because today was the school's *cultural festival*...apparently.

It was weird, though; I didn't remember helping to get ready for it. With cultural festivals, didn't the whole class work together in advance to prepare their contribution? Had they gotten all that out of the way while I was too busy dealing with a string of problems to come to school? Why hadn't anybody told me about it?

"Haaah..." I sighed a lonely sigh for my dull and drab school life...

"Sorry to keep you waiting," a girl said behind me.

The person I'd been waiting for had arrived. Grumbling that she was late, I turned around.

"You were the one who told me to come to this, and now you're la..."

I froze.

No, it wasn't because I had the wrong person. The one in front of me was definitely the girl I'd made that promise with; there was no question about that. The issue was—

"Siesta, what are you wearing...?"

What had arrested my attention was a bright white sailor uniform. She must have shortened the skirt somehow; it let me see her knees and a little more. She had a school bag slung over her shoulder, and anyone would've pegged her as one of our students... It was so different from the chic dress she usually wore, and between that and how good it looked, I just—

"? Why did you suddenly turn your back?" Siesta leaned over, peering into my face.

"...Uh, no reason. Just, uh, had some trouble breathing..."

"Does it hurt? Are you okay?"

I'm fine. I'm fine, so don't lean in so close, all right? And don't rub my back.

"...Why are you wearing our uniform?"

After I'd finally managed to calm down a bit, I asked her about that, squinting.

When I studied her more closely, I saw that she was wearing a red ribbon in her short, pale silver hair like a headband, as a fashion statement. *Okay, if I'm not extremely careful, I might slip and say she's cute or something, and that possibility is extremely...cute.*

"You know, your eyes are meaner than usual."

Ignore it. I just need a little more courage before I can take in your entire sailor-suited self at once.

Yeah, I actually hadn't calmed down at all.

To be fair, I wasn't overreacting: All the people who passed us were slowing down, fascinated by Siesta.

She was a beautiful girl with white hair and blue eyes in a sailor uniform. I completely understood why people would involuntarily whip out their cell phones... But the pictures'll cost you two trillion yen.

"I don't normally dress like this, so I decided to throw in a ribbon, too. What do you think?"

"If you want my impressions, I've already given enough to fill a page or so of a manuscript."

"Huh? When? I didn't hear it."

"More important...ahem."

"Oh, you mean why am I wearing a uniform?" Siesta twirled around once on her tiptoes. The wind made her skirt flare out, baring her thighs for a moment. I stared in spite of myself as Siesta leaned forward slightly, batting her lashes.

"I mean, don't you think a cultural festival date in school uniforms sounds like fun?"

She turned that smile and its hundred million watts of adorable on me.

"...Come to think of it, do I need a contract to become your assistant? Oh, and maybe a personal seal, to sign it..."

"Easy there, slow down. I shouldn't be the one saying this, but there are proper steps to follow. We still have some dialogue left when I'll try to talk you around, so hold on for a little while."

The school was bustling with local students, their parents and guardians, and students from other schools, and every classroom had been turned into a mock shop that sold things like crepes or takoyaki.

"All right, where should we start?" I asked Siesta for input, studying a flyer somebody in a full-body rabbit costume had handed me in the corridor. According to the flyer, they had a planetarium and a haunted house in addition to the festival stalls. And the haunted house was big—it took up a whole floor of the old school building, which wasn't normally used. It seemed pretty promising.

"That one's a must," she said.

"Yeah. We'll have to keep an eye on the schedule, though."

According to the flyer, the haunted house shut down for fifteen minutes every hour, probably so the staff could take breaks.

"Does that mean they won't accept customers outside those times?" Siesta asked the kid in the rabbit suit, although the answer seemed pretty obvious.

The bunny tilted its big head to the side, as if to say, "What are you even asking me?" I assumed it was trying to stay in character, which struck me as really professional. Well, the running shoes kinda killed the effect, but I guess it cared more about being able to walk easily.

"Hey, Siesta. It's written right here. They break for fifteen minutes."

"But according to the ideal route I just plotted in my head—"

"What, in that split second?"

"I don't think we'll be able to get to the old school building during the times written on this flyer." Apparently, Siesta's schedule had other priorities. "It would be better to fortify ourselves with some food first, you know?"

"So that's your goal, huh?"

"Like an hour-long, gigantamongous-portion eating challenge, maybe."

"Yeah, they're not going to be doing anything like that at a middle school cultural festival."

"And so," Siesta said, putting on her very best smile, "we'll be visiting outside regular hours, but please accommodate us anyway."

That was an unreasonable request for the bunny-suited student.

"Oh, there's a crepe stand!" As if to say her business was finished, Siesta set off toward one of the stalls up ahead.

"Siesta, listen, if you're gonna be unfair and dump work on people, at least dump it on me." I sighed, even as I caught up with her and bought a banana crepe on the spot.

"...? I didn't say anything, and you bought it for me anyway." Siesta seemed bewildered, but when I held the crepe out, she took a petite little bite. "You got mad at me earlier when I ordered the pizza. What happened?"

"Well, times change."

"Huh? But it's been barely any time at all. What's changed?"

Geez, she's not going to get it if I don't say it straight out, huh? Here goes nothing.

I turned to Siesta, who was staring at me, and I told her:

"I'll take the cultural festival in front of me over a Miss Hanako who doesn't even exist."

Mystery-horror? That stuff's not in style. The times call for—teen romantic comedy.

I put on the coolest expression I'd ever worn in my life.

"Haaah. Well, I'd never date you in a million years, so I'm not sure you could call this 'romantic comedy,' but..."

However, Siesta was not reacting the way I expected at all...

"Hmm?"

"Hmm?"

Although the school grounds were still bustling and lively, the world around me was suddenly very quiet. We stood there for a little while, gazing at each other, then tilted our heads in confusion.

Ah. Okay. Yes, okay, I get it.

"Huh? What? Kimi, you didn't think 'date' meant I was going to be your girlfriend, did you?"

Nope, not at all. Not by a single millimeter. Not the tiniest bit. I didn't, uh, think that. At all...

"Are you stupid, Kimi?"

"...Can we just erase the last paragraph or so from history?"

Hopefully I won't have to watch this scene again in a few years—I'd probably be writhing on the floor in embarrassment. Look, I'm a middle schooler, okay? Future me, have a heart and cut a guy some slack. Although I doubt that particular fear is something I'll ever have to worry about.

"Well, I prefer that version of you. It's easier to work with." Polishing off the crepe I was still holding, she said, "Let's go get some takoyaki next."

Taking my hand, she started off through the crowd.

"...You're gonna give some people the wrong idea, you know."

"Did you say something?"

"I said don't just walk into people's bathrooms."

"The only bathroom I invade without asking is yours."

"You're not gonna get me with that 'You're the only person I show this side of myself to' crap."

◆ This is when even atheists start praying

"Not fair."

All by myself in a dark cubicle, I was holding my head...well, my stomach, to be precise. Wave after wave of pain swept over me. The fierce struggle had been going on for more than ten minutes already, and I wiped sweat off my forehead.

"Dammit, this is all your fault, too, Siesta," I complained. She was probably chowing down on takoyaki again somewhere, right about now.

Basically, I was currently in a bathroom stall, battling stomach cramps.

The cause was clearly overeating, and that was entirely due to Siesta making me keep her company while she bought and consumed a ridiculous amount of food. Not only that, but when I'd asked her to let me rest a little, she'd ignored my request and dragged me around the haunted house in the old school building, and that was when the cramps had hit.

However, that wasn't the only reason I was feeling lousy. It was because this bathroom was actually located inside the haunted house—and the stall I was in was the one in the rumors: the third stall from the door in the girls' bathroom on the third floor of the old school building.

…No, wait, don't jump to conclusions. That's not it. This was the only stall that had been made available to the staff, guys and girls alike. They'd just let me use it because this was an emergency. I absolutely did not sneak into the girls' bathroom, all right?

Naturally, the inside of the bathroom was gloomy, and I'd been hearing eerie sounds in the background the whole time. Frankly, I wanted to get out of there ASAP…but my stomach was sounding a squeaky, gurgling alarm, as if warning me to stay on the john. To put it mildly:

"I want to die."

And so here I was.

To make matters worse, the ominous atmosphere kept the rumor going through my mind despite my desire to keep it at bay.

"I mean, come on, I'm in middle school. There's no way ghosts and monsters still freak me out."

"Who are you making excuses to?"

"…!"

A voice that wasn't mine came from somewhere above me, and I froze… but it was a girl's voice, one I'd heard somewhere before.

"What, peeping at me in the bath wasn't enough for you? Don't peep while I'm on the toilet, Siesta."

When I looked up, there she was. She'd climbed up on the stall door and was peering down at me. I thought she'd headed for the exit on her own, but no, she'd come back. Sighing, I pulled up my pants. The darkness had worked in my favor; I was pretty sure she hadn't quite managed to see anything.

"You were taking so long, I got worried… And down we go."

"What? No. Why did you get down?"

"Was I supposed to stay up there forever?"

"No, get down on the *outside*." Why had she gone out of her way to climb down in here with me?

"There's something I want to check... Mm, found it." Siesta bent down and retrieved something from the shadows around the toilet. It was a scrap of plastic, maybe from a bag.

"What do you think this is?"

"Let's see... Maybe it's from a bag of cold medicine? Like, maybe somebody took it after they ate their lunch in here."

"The fact that that's the very first thing you thought of makes me feel pure sympathy for you. Don't tell me this 'peaceful routine' you want to protect involves you eating your lunch all by yourself in the bathroom."

"As I told you, my parents are missing. Present progressive tense. So nobody's ever made me lunch. The only lunch I eat in the bathroom is sweet rolls."

"Okay, I really feel bad for you now. Shall I make you lunch every once in a while?"

After dropping that on me as if it were nothing:

"Hup."

Reaching under her skirt, Siesta hooked her fingers onto *something* and started to pull down.

"Siesta, wait! Can't you see me here?! You know I can see you, right?!"

"Huh? That's a very dubious habit you've got, making a girl hold it when she needs to go."

"I didn't say that... I said absolutely nothing even remotely like that."

"Anyway, I'm going to tinkle, so leave, Kimi."

"Huh? You're planning to toss me out into this creepy place by myself?"

"Weren't you just telling yourself, 'I mean, come on, I'm in middle school. There's no way ghosts and monsters still freak me out'? With your pants around your ankles?"

"If you saw, then you should've reacted back then!"

This couldn't be right. We were in a teen rom-com at the cultural festival; how had we ended up acting out a comedy routine in the bathroom of a haunted house? Although, if you took the words "haunted house" and "comedy routine" in isolation, you could say we were still making the most of the cultural festival...

I sighed, and that was when it happened.

"Quiet." Siesta put a hand over my mouth.

I strained my ears, wondering what was going on, and then—*tap-tap-tap*.

Somebody knocked on the door of our stall.

No way, I thought. We were currently in the third stall from the door of the girls' bathroom on the third floor of the old school building. It wasn't three in the morning, but there were more than enough conditions in place to remind me of that rumor.

It happened again: *tap-tap-tap*.

Whoever it was knocked a second time. Siesta and I nodded to each other. Slowly, we unlocked the door and pushed it open, and in the next instant—

"...! ...Hmm?"

Outside the stall was a girl in a red jumper skirt—er, scratch that. Somebody in a pink rabbit suit.

"Weren't you handing out flyers in the school?"

No, wait, had that been a panda? I had seen multiple students in full-body character suits, handing out flyers or carrying directory signs around.

Anyway, what was this rabbit doing here?

Oh, were they a haunted house staff member? Maybe they'd come because we'd been in here so long that they'd gotten worried. If so, I'd have to think up a good excuse. What kind of white lie would convince someone who'd just caught a girl and guy together in a bathroom stall—?

"I won't let you get away."

However, I promptly realized that I wouldn't have time to think up any excuse, and that there wouldn't have been any point anyway.

The next thing I knew, the person in the bunny suit had turned tail and hared off—and Siesta was *pointing a gun at their back*.

"Hey, Siesta...?"

With no clue what was going on, I just stood there, but Siesta launched into a run. As she took off, she called back to me:

"That bunny is Miss Hanako of the Toilet."

◆ A pure-white dress and the flying bride

"Hurry," Siesta called.

Even though I still had no idea what was happening, I chased after the bunny suit, too. It didn't have much of a lead on us yet. I'd assumed we'd catch it right away, but…

"Who'd have thought they'd be this fast…"

Come to think of it, I remembered that rabbit had been wearing high-performance athletic shoes. They couldn't have factored this chase into their plans beforehand, could they?

"Whoa!"

To make matters worse, my foot caught on something and I stumbled. When I shone my phone screen on it to see what it was…it turned out to be a fake severed head. Ah, right—this entire floor was a haunted house. There wasn't much light, and the complicated, maze-like layout was slowing us down more than we'd anticipated.

"Geez. This is kid stuff." Sighing, I straightened up. "So what do you mean, 'That bunny is Miss Hanako'?"

"I'll explain later. Right now, get moving as fast as you can."

"It's pretty hard to make myself chase somebody when I don't understand why I'm doing it."

"I'm telling you, we don't have that kind of time. And why are you squeezing my hand?"

Dammit. She caught me, huh? I thought I'd be okay if I did it casually.

"What, do you like me, Kimi?"

"Are you an idiot?"

"Wow, that is incredibly irritating."

"I just grabbed your hand involuntarily because that severed head on the ground scared me. Obviously."

"That's nothing to brag about. You're being far more unfair than me right now."

"Ha-ha! I win."

During that stupid exchange, we got out of the haunted house. Then we crossed the long corridor that linked the old school building with the new one, which put us back among the mock shops. However…

"This is, uh…"

There, we found multiple people in bunny costumes, handing out flyers and balloons in the crowded corridor. It wasn't possible to tell which was *the real one* at a glance.

"No better place to hide a tree than in the forest, hmm? …Nom-nom."

"Yeah, they lost us real good. Wait, are you eating?" When I looked over at Siesta, she was munching on a buttered baked potato. "Seriously? Now? You're the one who started this whole chase; if anybody needs to keep their guard up, it's you."

"I can't move unless I refuel. And they want three hundred yen for this."

"You were gonna explode a few minutes ago. And don't just send me the bill again."

"Okay, you can have a bite, so let's split the check."

"Check-splitting. Wow. Oh, hey, isn't that the one?"

On the opposite side of the U-shaped school building, I'd spotted someone in a rabbit costume gazing at us from a distance, through the window. They darted off, as if they'd noticed me looking back.

"That was dumb. If they had just played it cool, we never would've guessed. All right, let's go catch 'em."

"I really like the way you eventually decided to just go with the flow. Continue to develop that trait."

"I told you, that's annoying. I have not agreed to an assistant training project."

As we bantered with each other, we broke into a run again. And just then—

"This is the Costuming Club! Come try on costumes for free!" a girl called, trying to attract visitors.

If we'd had time, I would have liked to enjoy the sight of Siesta as a cat-eared maid for a little while, but sadly, we didn't.

"Two, please."

Or apparently we did.

"No, we don't! Seriously! They're going to get away again!"

Siesta was headed into the classroom, and I caught the cuff of her sleeve.

"This is our strategy. If our opponent is going to blend into a sea of character costumes, we'll disguise ourselves with cosplay."

"Is that actually going to work? I get the feeling a cat-eared maid would draw a lot of attention."

"Oh, come on, it's fine... And why are you assuming I'd be a cat-eared maid? I'm not wearing that."

Soon we were ushered into the classroom, handed bags with costumes in them, then shown into simple changing rooms that had been partitioned off. Alone behind the curtain, I took my costume out of its bag.

"...Uh..."

Frankly, I wouldn't exactly go out of my way to wear this... Any middle schooler would have found it a little embarrassing. Still, if the goal was to disguise ourselves, it had to be done. After hesitating a little, I pulled on the costume, steeled myself, and opened the curtain.

"...And nobody's even looking."

This after I'd braced myself and everything. Jerks.

So what were the Costuming Club members doing? For some reason, they were all gathered around the other changing room, squealing. The person inside was, naturally, the one who'd come in with me.

"Sorry to keep you waiting."

When the curtain finally opened, *there was Siesta in a pure-white wedding dress.*

"How is it?" Smiling, she tilted her head gently.

"Oh, uh. Well...... It looks good on you," I managed to say, tearing my eyes away.

"...I didn't think you'd actually tell me."

"Well, I mean, there's no point in lying."

"You look good, too, Kimi... That tuxedo suits you." Siesta pointed at my outfit.

"I-it does, huh?"

"Yes..."

We were both refusing to look at each other now. This was terribly awkward.

"If you'd like, I'll take a photo for you!" One of the Costuming Club girls held up a camera.

"Well, I guess...?"

"Since we're here..."

We glanced at each other again, then accepted the offer.

"All right, are you ready? Say cheese!"

Click.

The traditional peace sign pose didn't seem appropriate to our clothes, so the photo only showed Siesta and me, standing side by side. The girl sent it to each of our smartphones.

"This will be a good memory, huh?" Siesta said bashfully, and I smiled faintly.

Yeah, it really was—

"—Wait, no!!"

I yelled.

"The rabbit! We're chasing the rabbit, remember?!"

Why on earth had we let this cosplay thing fry our brains? We'd completely forgotten our main goal...

"We accidentally used up too much of our runtime on the romantic comedy, didn't we? Let's hurry."

Finally, Siesta was back to her usual self, and she sprinted out of the classroom, still wearing the wedding dress.

"Hey! ...Argh, dammit. We'll bring the costumes back later!" I called to the dazed Costuming Club members, then managed to catch up to Siesta somehow.

"Not exactly made for running," she said.

"You're definitely the only person on the planet who'd play tag dressed like that."

A girl and guy in a wedding dress and tuxedo dashed down the long corridor. Every student there whipped out their smartphone. Did they think we were doing a cosplay event or something? If those photos ended up on social media, this was going to haunt me forever.

"Hey..." Siesta was wearing a smile sunny enough to blow those gloomy clouds away. "This is fun, isn't it, Assistant?"

That smile she was giving me, right then, was exactly what people mean when they talk about the joy of youth.

"Who are you calling your assistant?"

"Oh, you caught that, huh?"

Don't give me that. And don't flip right back to normal. Geez.

"Assistant, over there." Siesta pointed toward the window. Beyond it, I saw...

"It ran all that way?"

The bunny suit was cutting straight across the schoolyard, through the teeming crowd.

"They actually stayed in the bunny costume for us. What a conscientious fugitive."

"You can't get out of those by yourself."

"Well, now I feel bad for it." Running full tilt in that costume at this time of year? It had to be sweating buckets.

"That's why we have to be humane and catch it fast," Siesta said as she flung open the window.

"...Whoa, wait, I've got a really bad feeling about this. I'm pretty sure I'm wrong, but you're not planning to jump from here, are you?"

"No, I'm not."

Okay. Phew.

"It's not just me. You're coming, too."

"Huh?"

"It's fine. The shoes I'm wearing are one of those Seven Tools I was telling you about, meaning—"

No sooner had she spoken than Siesta scooped me up, set a foot on the windowsill, and—

"—they let me fly."

That day, the photo of a girl in a wedding dress holding a guy in a tuxedo in her arms and leaping into the sky blew up on social media.

◆ And so the unforgettable adventure began

"So that bunny really was one of the Miss Hanakos of the Toilet?"

The next day, at a certain café...

Siesta and I were discussing the facts behind the recent incident.

"That's right. This is from the *drugs* the students who'd stopped coming to school were taking."

After pausing for a sip of black tea, Siesta took the transparent bag from the folds of her skirt and set it on the table. It was what she'd picked up in the girls' bathroom on the third floor of the old school building yesterday.

"It resembles a type of stimulant. It gives a temporary euphoric sensation and boosts your concentration. At this school, it looks as though it started with the track and field team, then spread."

"I had no idea… Then you mean the students who are skipping were using that drug?"

"Yes. After all, such a remarkable effect comes with some pretty incredible side effects. Memory trouble, in particular. It'll probably take quite a while for them to recover completely."

"I see…"

On the bright side, though, recovery *was* possible, through a regimen of careful treatments. You could probably call that the one silver lining here.

"Then the fact that the Miss Hanakos were multiplying means…"

"It was probably because the drug was highly habit-forming. In order to get the money to buy more, they started to sell it themselves… I think that's how the Miss Hanakos multiplied more and more rapidly."

An illegal drug that could only be bought at the third stall from the door of the girls' bathroom on the third floor of the old school building. The rumor about Miss Hanako of the Toilet had been used as a code for those secret transactions. Of course, the number of students who'd known what it actually meant had probably been limited, but a few of them had been using that urban legend as a cover to commit crimes.

"As a matter of fact, I hear that drug is based on a pollen-like substance produced by a certain plant."

"So that's why it was 'Miss *Hanako*,' huh? 'Flower child.' What a dumb joke."

But that weak pun had created a shadow that had victimized multiple people.

I hadn't noticed the situation at all. I'd said that all I needed was for my days to be quiet and monotonous, and yet the flower-poison had already been eating away at that peaceful routine.

"Wait, wasn't Miss Hanako only supposed to appear at three in the morning? What was she doing at a cultural festival in broad daylight?"

"It just goes to show how desperate *they* were. They were watching for a chance to steal a march on their *rivals* and spread their drug around."

"I see. That rabbit was one of them, then?"

Thanks to the guilt of using illegal drugs, the Miss Hanakos had found it hard to go out in public. However, at the cultural festival, they'd be able to blend into the crowd. Not only that, but they'd probably assumed they wouldn't be noticed if they used full-body costumes to hide their identities.

"Siesta, you knew something was off about that rabbit right from the start, didn't you?"

"Yes. After all, going out of their way to wear *a character suit with running shoes* was practically broadcasting their identity."

Oh, right. I had heard that a lot of the Miss Hanakos were on the track team. So Siesta had known the bunny was actually a drug-pushing track team member the moment she ran into it? The running shoes they'd worn, just in case they needed to flee, had ended up working against them.

"Then you slyly dropped *a code word*, established contact with the rabbit, and pretended you were a *client*."

Come to think of it, when Siesta had first accepted the flyer from the rabbit, she'd really emphasized being *outside normal hours*. She hadn't been talking about the haunted house's breaks. She'd meant a drug transaction at a time other than three in the morning. Then the rabbit had come straight to the site, but when they'd seen Siesta holding a gun, they'd realized it was a trap and bolted.

"First-rate detectives resolve incidents before they even occur, you see."

I'd heard that line before.

As she sipped her tea, Siesta gave an elegant wink.

"Well, I guess it wasn't much of a case for you, huh?"

After all, Siesta was an ace detective who fought in bitter, large-scale battles with pseudohumans. She could probably handle illicit drug deals before breakfast...*before her afternoon siesta.*

"However, I did hear that a certain organization was involved with the flower from this incident."

"'A certain organization'? You can't mean..."

Wordlessly, Siesta nodded.

The secret society SPES. Of course. Where there were drugs, there was a boss—a mastermind. Before I'd even noticed, their shadows had stretched right into my neighborhood.

"So?" Setting her cup down on its saucer, Siesta looked at me. "What are you going to do?"

Her blue gaze caught me, and it wouldn't let go.

I didn't have to ask what she meant.

She wanted to know if I was prepared. If I was going to climb out of my lukewarm bath, which was stone-cold now, and throw myself into combat. That was the silent question in her eyes.

In that case…

"Siesta."

…I asked her a question of my own.

"If I become your assistant, what's in it for me? What can you provide?"

That was the starting point of this discussion, which I'd suggested. But I knew it was pointless to ask that.

I'd caught on now.

Why are you insisting on me? Why am I the one who has to be your assistant? It's because I get dragged into things. As long as you have that, incidents and trouble will come find you on their own.

Siesta was pursuing cases—or SPES, to be precise—and to her, I was the best human resource ever. The ace detective didn't want an assistant; she wanted cases.

She wasn't looking at me at all. Whatever she was about to offer me would be a bunch of random things she pulled out of the air. My questions had been asked with spiteful intentions, and I'd already decided to turn her down once I knew what the answers were.

Siesta squeezed her eyes shut tightly, and then…

"I'll protect you."

…she opened them again, smiling softly as she went on.

"No matter what kind of trouble finds you, I'll protect you with my life. And so…" she said.

"Kimi— Be my assistant."

Siesta held her left hand out to me, across the table.

"…Look at you, trying to swindle me into this."

Naturally, I wasn't about to take her up on that all-surface, no-substance proposal—

"Well, if you're going to go that far, I suppose I could go along with you."

—or so I thought, but the next thing I knew, I'd taken her hand.

Why, you ask? How the hell should I know? I'd like to ask somebody myself.

But for some reason…no matter how hard I tried, I just couldn't get that picture out of my mind—the sight of her leaping into the sky, wearing something she was ten years too young for.

"After all that complaining, now you're suddenly warm to the idea. I've never seen such an obvious male *tsundere* in my life."

"Don't pigeonhole your assistant into a random category."

"You're already acknowledging yourself as my assistant."

"—Ghk. Figure of speech."

"Actually, we already had our answer when you showed up *here,* didn't we?" Siesta fluttered two airline tickets at me.

Yes, I should mention that the café we were sitting in was the airport lounge.

"…And what is an assistant to you, anyway? You keep throwing the word around."

"Hmm. How about you wake me up every morning, say, and make me brush my teeth, and dress me?"

"…………That's a hard no."

"You thought about it for quite a while, though. Did you think you might like that life?"

"Argh, shut up! I get it, all right?! As you wish: I'll be your assistant!"

Then I smacked the table, stood up, and—

"So stay with me as long as I live!"

—lost control of my emotions and said what I was actually feeling.

"Huh? Did you just propo—?"

"No! I take it back!"

Interlude 1

"…Uh, what exactly was that story for?"

Hang on. Especially that last bit; what was that?

I'd thought she was starting pretty far back, and then she'd busted out an especially embarrassing episode for me. Weren't these supposed to reveal the truth behind Siesta's death? This one had just been a trap to humiliate me…

"Oops, wrong one."

"That was absolutely on purpose!"

Siesta, who'd appeared on the screen again, lowered her head slightly. Her face was still expressionless.

Seriously, don't set up ways to mess with me a year in advance…

…That said, thinking back, that was how Siesta and I had decided that it was in both our best interests to stick together before we set off on our journey.

"Rgh! Why did Ma'am choose an underhanded guy like Kimizuka instead of me?"

"Calm down, Charlie. That was four years ago; what's the point of getting jealous now? And don't insult me just because you can."

"Ghk! How come the two of you had already promised to get married years ago…?"

"Calm down, Natsunagi. Why would *you* be jealous, too?"

"Haaah, you really are a child, Kimizuka," Saikawa said. "You don't understand girls' feelings."

"Says the youngest one here."

Come on, this is turning into a routine—one person says something dumb, everybody starts in, and it doesn't stop until they all run out of material? I don't have the stamina to shut all of this down…

"All right, I really am going to show you an important incident that connects to the truth of my death next, but—before I do that, I'll give the four of you a hint," Siesta explained to us. "Don't misread individual pieces of information. Keep track of who's saying what at the moment. And always doubt what you're seeing. I want you to remember that from now on."

"Doubt what we see..." Natsunagi murmured softly. Then she glanced at me. "Huh? Maybe this isn't really Kimizuka...?"

"I know Siesta had that thing about forgetting what I look like if she hadn't seen me for two days, but you can let that one lie. You don't have to honor *everything* from her last wish."

And that is absolutely not what she meant by that, all right?

"Now that that's out of the way, I'll show the next clip," Siesta said. On the screen, the scene changed. "My assistant should still remember this part as well."

The screen showed the streets of London.

Siesta and I were just entering a brick building.

"I'm pretty sure this is..."

A little over a year ago. I recognized the building where we'd lived and had our office. And what had happened in this city—

"All right, here we go."

Siesta signaled that the story was about to move forward.

"From this point on, try to uncover the truth of my death."

Chapter 2

◆ And thus the dead rise again

"Jack the Ripper is back from the dead. I want you to help us bring him in."

London, England.

In the office where Siesta and I had taken up residence, Ms. Fuubi sat on the sofa opposite us, smoking.

"...Ms. Fuubi, what are you doing in England?"

"Well, I hadn't told you two, but they sent me here on loan. That contract ended yesterday, though; I'll be heading back to Japan on the next flight."

"I never heard they were reshuffling personnel that way..."

Fuubi Kase was an acquaintance from Japan, a redheaded police officer. However, I hadn't seen her in person for a bit under three years, not since I left Japan with Siesta.

She'd shown up without an appointment just a few minutes ago, skipped the part where she said hello after so many years apart, and thrown a request at us about Jack the Ripper.

"There's no smoking here."

"Shut up."

So unfair.

"So, I'm handing this case off to you two. Catch him, all right?"

"You mean the, um..."

Jack the Ripper, otherwise known as the Whitechapel Murderer, was the name of the culprit behind a series of murders that had taken place in England in 1888. The culprit had never been identified, and even now, a hundred years later, the singularity of the incident still drew considerable interest.

"Yeah, that's the guy. There've been a lot of incidents using his M.O. lately, here in London. A corpse turned up today, even."

The same M.O., huh? If I remembered right, Jack the Ripper had been famous for his grotesque methods, cutting his victims' bodies apart and extracting their organs. That said—

"But the incident's over a hundred years old, right? The guy's dead."

"Yeah, that's why I said *he's come back to life.*"

"That's just crazy."

Dead people never come back to life. Even grade school kids know that.

...In which case...

"It's a modern-day Jack the Ripper? A *copycat*?" I asked Ms. Fuubi, who was still blowing smoke through rouged lips.

"You're taking this so damn seriously. But yeah, that's probably it."

"Then just start with that, would you?"

"The young lady over there wouldn't take an interest in it unless I put it the other way." Ms. Fuubi narrowed her eyes at the ace detective, who was conked out on her desk.

"Hey, Siesta. She's talking smack about you."

Siesta was resting her forehead on the desk. I shook her a few times... but she didn't even flinch. Now that she'd gotten started on a nap, I guessed that it would take more than this to wake her up. In that case—

"Dodge or die, Siesta." I got up, grabbed a carving knife from the kitchen behind us, and threw it at her.

"...That's not safe."

Still with her face on the desk, Siesta caught the tip of the blade between her fingers. Then she stretched melodramatically and sat up.

"Are you wired to not wake up unless you're in mortal danger?" I asked, plopping down on the sofa with exasperation.

"It's your fault for giving me the opportunity to nap."

"This isn't about opportunity. Sometimes you fall asleep when you're eating. Are you an infant?"

"Huh? You're the baby, aren't you, Kimi? That game you play, sometimes..."

"We have a guest. Shut your mouth, right this second."

Listen. Forget what we just said immediately. I mean it.

"So, what was it again? Jack the Ripper has revived in the present?" Siesta gave a small, cat-like yawn, directing her question at me.

"How did you manage to listen to that conversation in your sleep? Also, you've got marks on your forehead."

"My acoustic cells are always working, even when I'm asleep... You're kidding, where? Are they red?"

"Ugh, you sound like Bat. Here, use your hand mirror and look."

"At least I haven't sprouted a creepy tentacle. Wow, it looks like a pattern."

"Ha-ha! You look like a little kid when you push your hair up. Your forehead's wider than I figured."

"Oh, shut up. You're one of those people who's going to end up bald. Your hair is incredibly fine, too."

"Hey! Don't start touching it. Get off me... Take that!"

"Ow! Well, you've certainly got guts. Flick my forehead, will you?"

With a belligerent smile, Siesta lunged at me, and—

"So when did this kind of relationship start?"

Rolling her eyes, Ms. Fuubi blew cigarette smoke. She was watching me and Siesta, who was sitting on my lap.

"I don't know what you mean by 'relationship.'"

"We're just regular, um..." I looked at the girl on my lap, and she looked back at me.

""Business partners,"" we said in unison. The facts were obvious.

I mean, it's me and Siesta, okay? We couldn't possibly be anything else.

Before long, Ms. Fuubi stood up, as if she'd lost interest in her own question. "Well, it's not like I care," she said, stubbing out her cigarette. "Hurry up and go meet the victim."

FUU
(PHOO)

◆ Mysteries really should be littered with corpses

"This is the work of Cerberus."

Siesta had crouched down and was gazing at a man's bloodied corpse.

We were inside a baroque church building—that was where the present-day Jack the Ripper had committed his murder. Ms. Fuubi hadn't come with us, but the police had made an exception for us, let us across the tape, and allowed us to examine the scene of the murder. However—

"Cerberus?" I asked, puzzled. That didn't seem to fit with the situation.

"Your voice sounds weird."

"I'm not great with the smell of blood."

"Why don't you at least pick one? Either tilt your head or hold your nose," Siesta said. "Look." She held up one of the Seven Tools—a small hand mirror—which she wore at her waist.

I see. Yes, the guy in the reflection was striking a very bizarre pose.

Following Siesta's advice, I switched to just holding my nose, then crouched down beside her.

In the back of the chapel, beneath a large cross, lay the body of a dead man who seemed to have been a member of the clergy.

"Don't touch it."

"I know that. I won't leave fingerprints."

"Spoken like a criminal."

"Then this case will be closed real quick." Even as I swapped jokes with her, I put my hands together.

After a few seconds of silent prayer, I opened my eyes. No matter how many times you see corpses, you never get used to them. Over the past seventeen years of random trouble, I'd seen my fair share of death. Still, the stink of blood in the air and the clouded eyes of the dead always really messed with my head.

"And? You're saying this Cerberus is the real identity of the new Jack the Ripper?" I asked, squinting at the ghastly scene.

Once again, I saw the corpse of a priest with a gaping hole in the left side of his chest.

"Yes. That's his code name. He's the guard dog of Hades, and they say he devours human hearts." Siesta brushed her hair behind her ear, her expression as cool as always.

"So you're saying it's *them*?"

"I can't be absolutely sure yet, but…" Siesta put a fingertip to her jaw. "I'll admit, it might have been different a century ago— When they've committed this many murders in a row, but the police still don't have even a hint of a lead…"

"Well, yeah, I can guess."

As I'd thought, the enemy was SPES— And if our suspect had a code name, he had to be a pseudohuman.

"What's the enemy's objective? Why is Cerberus going around stealing hearts?"

He couldn't possibly just be imitating Jack the Ripper, could he?

"It's hard to imagine that he's been doing this independently. He must be acting on orders from the top."

Orders from the top… If I recalled, the hijacking incident where Siesta and I had met three years ago had also been committed on orders from Bat's organization.

"Well, we can make the enemy tell us all about their objective when we capture him."

"Siesta, you look like you might torture him with a straight face."

"Don't say things that will make me look bad. Oh, or did you say that because you wanted me to do that to you?"

"Yeah right. Is this your way of conditioning me?"

Anyway, this wasn't a conversation we should be having at a murder scene.

"You said we could make him spill it when we captured him, but…do you have any idea how we're going to do that?"

He'd already killed several people. If even the police weren't able to do anything, how was she planning to get him?

"…What's *that thing* you've got?" Instead of answering my question, Siesta glanced at my hands.

"Oh, this? Ms. Fuubi gave it to me to hang on to when we went our separate ways back there." I clicked the Zippo lighter I'd taken out of my pocket, fidgeting with it. "She said she was going to quit smoking, so I could have it."

I didn't know where the change of heart had come from, but it would be nice not to have to worry about her smoking in my house.

"I see. So after years apart, she entrusted her most precious possession to a young man."

"What sort of emotion is that supposed to be?"

After all, as far as Ms. Fuubi's concerned, I'm just a suspicious kid she keeps running into at murder scenes.

…And this wasn't the time for a stupid conversation anyway.

"Look, about capturing Cerberus. Do you have a plan?"

If we just stood by and watched, the victims would keep piling up. We had to act as soon as we possibly could.

"As a matter of fact, I've been aware of the damage Cerberus is doing for a while now." Siesta crouched down again, looking at the corpse with the missing heart.

"Well, there's no way you'd miss an incident this big."

Even if there was no job request involved, Siesta stuck to her mission and fought the "enemies of the world." That was just who she was. Which meant there had to be a reason she hadn't been able to catch Cerberus so far.

"The enemy seems to have a good nose. I've tried getting close several times, but he always slips away."

"I see. That's a dog for you, I guess."

Just as Bat's ears had been highly developed, most pseudohumans' bodies were reinforced in one area or another. In Cerberus's case, his nose was apparently his star feature.

"And yet Cerberus is still committing his crimes, even though we're here in London, too."

"…You think it's a trap?"

"I was going to say it was a chance." The ace detective was as confident as always. "True, he could be plotting something. However, if we let this opportunity get away, we may never find another decent chance to capture him."

"Okay, but how specifically do you plan to go after him?"

"You've got it backward." Siesta stood up. "We're not going after Cerberus. Cerberus is coming after us."

She didn't appear to be joking, but what she was saying didn't make much sense.

"Listen. From the enemy's perspective, this is a chance to defeat us."

"But Cerberus ran because he was scared of you, right? So—" Suddenly, I had a sneaking suspicion I wouldn't like where this was going. "Whoa, Siesta, you can't mean..."

"You've gotten pretty *good at making deductions,* too." Siesta grinned. "I'm the only one Cerberus is afraid of. Meaning if you're on your own, the enemy will waltz right in to attack you."

"So you really are planning to make me be a decoy?!"

This detective wants to use me as bait for hell's guard dog!

"You must have known this time would come at some point after you took this job."

"I have no memory of bracing for death!"

Dammit, what happened to the part where she said she'd protect me?!

"Your time has come, Kimi. Now you will fight a mighty enemy, too."

"Don't set me up as some legendary hero."

"No, I'm the legendary hero. At most, you're the sword I use to slash apart my enemies...or maybe the owner of the smithy where it was forged... No, actually, the character who didn't succeed to that guy's position and became a farmer instead, maybe?"

"You are so unfair."

What an awful way to treat her assistant, especially when he was about to confront a monstrous evil all by himself.

"Well, we should get going. I've got everything I need from the scene." Without so much as glancing at me or the unhappy look on my face, Siesta spun to face the exit.

"...Where are we going next?"

"Hmm, maybe a preliminary meeting over afternoon tea?"

"You are the only person on the planet who could go straight from a murder scene to afternoon tea."

This ace detective was slim, but she ate as heartily as ever. In London, she was constantly polishing off Sunday roasts at restaurants. We had to work like crazy just to cover the food expenses.

"...I'm constantly overworking my brain, so my three great drives are a bit stronger than most people's." Siesta turned back to me and started speaking much faster than normal.

It was rare to see her like this.

Apparently, she was equipped with the same sensibilities as the average girl.

"Is that why you're always taking naps?" I asked.

"Says the one who always wakes up cranky."

Lobbing nonsense at each other, we put that place behind us.

"So, if your three great drives are stronger than other people's…"

"…I only meant hunger and sleep, actually."

◆ The ace detective doesn't arrive late

"All right, just relax in your room, Kimi. Eat pizza or something and enjoy what's left of your lif— I mean, leisure time."

"You are coming to save me, right? You're gonna come to the rescue before he kills me, right?"

I was in a hotel room Siesta had arranged for. We'd finished our afternoon tea meeting, then had dinner. Now that I'd parted with Siesta, I was lying on the bed by myself, talking to her on the phone. We were running through the final confirmation of our strategy: the one where I was going to be the bait for Cerberus.

"It's been almost three years since I started traveling the world with you. It went by so quickly…"

"Don't suddenly start waxing nostalgic about the past. We can do our reminiscing when we're both a lot older."

"At first, all we did was fight…and I suppose that hasn't changed. Still, life was never boring with you around."

"Stop acting like I'm gonna die!"

I may be her assistant, but I'm not planning to donate my life, all right?

"…And? Cerberus is actually going to come to this room, isn't he?"

Unfortunately, I'd signed on for this maneuver already, and I couldn't back out now. Meaning I should probably switch gears and start getting ready, to raise our chances of success.

"It'll be fine. If this goes the way I think it will, Cerberus will chew you up around midnight tonight."

"So I am gonna die, huh?"

Seriously, come save me. Please. Be punctual. Come early, even.

"Well, uh, guess I've got less than three hours left to live, then."

When I stole a glance out the window, it was already completely dark outside.

"To be honest, I'm not sure of the time, and I don't even know whether it's going to happen today."

…Yeah, I guess not. All we knew was that Cerberus would likely come after me, now that I'd split up with Siesta; it wasn't like we had the date and time nailed down. I'd probably end up on standby in this hotel room until he showed up.

"Are you checked into the room next door or something, Siesta?"

"Are you stupid, Kimi?"

She didn't have to say that. Unfair.

"If I'm nearby, the enemy will be too wary to make a move."

…Oh yeah. Good point, actually.

"Hang on. You mean I'm really, genuinely alone? You're sure I'm not actually going to die today?"

"It's fine. I have technically taken steps, so there's a minuscule chance you'll be saved."

"Just minuscule?"

"I'm kidding. Geez."

The trouble is, with you, it never sounds like a joke. "Haaah, I wish you were in the room with me…"

Imagining the worst-case scenario, I sighed in spite of myself. At that—

"……Hmm?" The voice from the telephone took on a teasing quality. *"So you wanted to spend the night with me."*

"—! That's not what I meant. Just in terms of physical safety."

"You wanted to share a bed with me."

"I told you, that's not it. Besides, you sleep rough; just how many times do you think you've hit me with a back-fist?"

"Then you wanted to take a bath together?"

"Your baths last forever. I can't hang out with you that long."

"You never say what you mean when it comes to these things."

Unfortunately, that is what I mean.

"I kinda just don't care anymore… Okay, I should go."

The inane exchange had drained any motivation I had to care about this. I'd just gamble on those steps Siesta had said she'd taken. I started to hang up, but just then…

"Siesta, are you outside?"

From the receiver, I thought I'd heard a distant car horn.

"Huh? Well, yes, but…"

"Go back to the apartment before it gets too late. Cerberus isn't the only dangerous type around."

"……"

For some reason, there was silence on the line.

"Siesta?"

"…Ah, sorry. It was just novel to have you treating me like a girl, so—"

"You were startled?"

"I laughed."

"Oh, you did, huh?"

Well, don't. Jerk.

See what happens the moment I show her a little kindness?

"All right, I'm hanging up."

"I can't go near you, but I'll at least leave the line open, so you don't get lonely."

"I'm not lonely or anything… But, I mean, if you really, *really* want to keep the line open, then I guess I could—"

"Yes, okay, okay. You don't have to say the rest; I get it."

A few hours passed. The more unwelcome a hunch or prediction is, the more likely it is to be right on target. What exactly was that prediction, you ask? That would be the time we'd predicted Cerberus would attack.

—I felt someone in the room with me.

According to my vague internal clock, it was a little past midnight.

I should have been alone. Just now, though, I was sure I'd sensed something moving nearby.

It had been several hours since that phone call. I'd been killing time by ordering room service and watching TV. Then I'd turned out the lights and gotten into bed, although I hadn't changed out of my clothes. Pretending to be asleep, I'd waited, bracing myself for that extremely unlikely possibility…and apparently, I'd lucked out.

The enemy was probably alone.

I'd turned off all the lights, so it was very dark and very quiet. I couldn't even hear the air conditioning. And then, just now, my ears had definitely caught the sound of a pistol's safety being released. Somebody was making an attempt on my life. However—

"Sorry. I'm used to *almost getting killed*."

To a certain extent, I could sense where my opponent was. Leaping up from the bed to catch them off guard, I trapped their gun arm between my legs in a cross lock.

"……—!"

It was my life, and I'd defend it myself.

Yes, I was counting on Siesta as a last resort, but I'd do what I could do on my own. Trouble had been finding me for as long as I could remember, so I'd acquired a certain level of proficiency in martial arts to deal with it. Lately, Siesta had trained me even more.

"You're gonna end up with a broken bone or two, all right?" *Sorry, but I show no mercy to pseudohumans.*

"—……!"

The gun fell from the enemy's hand, but I didn't release my hold. Siesta wasn't nearby, and I had to buy her enough time to get here.

"Don't move. You'll only hurt… Uh, wha—?"

Suddenly, I couldn't feel the upper arm in my hold anymore, and then—

"Ghk, hah…!"

A sharp pain ran through my face. I bit my tongue, and the taste of iron immediately filled my mouth.

"…What, you dislocated your own shoulder?"

It was dark, so I couldn't actually see them, but I was pretty sure I was right. They'd pulled their right arm out of its socket, then flipped their whole body to land a solid kick on my face. Not a move for your average human.

"Ha-ha. I guess it wouldn't be, huh?"

No "average human" here. This was Cerberus, Hades' heart-devouring guard dog—and the revenant Jack the Ripper.

"Well, Siesta, I bought you thirty seconds."

Pinning my hopes on my partner, although I had no idea where she even was, I took a step, then swung my right leg. I was aiming for the gun the enemy had dropped. My leg cut through empty space; I'd come so close, too.

"Damn…"

He'd picked it up first. Then I heard a gunshot and felt the bullet whiz right past my cheek.

"So you don't care how you kill me, huh, as long as the job gets done?"

Was he planning to slash through my chest and take my heart afterward?

I ducked down as low as I could, taking cover. I was at a disadvantage when it came to weapons, and without the ability to see, there was nothing else I could do. There had to be something I could do—

Oh. Guess I still had this.

"That's a police officer for you. It's like she saw this coming."

I still had the Zippo in the right-hand pocket of my trousers. I pulled it out, lit it, and flung it onto the bed.

"…!"

The fire blazed up, spreading in the blink of an eye…until the sprinklers in the ceiling came on.

"Gotcha."

"……!"

The enemy had recoiled, startled by the jets of water, and I shoved him down onto the bed.

"Game over."

Sorry, Siesta. It looks like I won't be needing you this time.

"All right, let's see who you really are."

I reached for the light switch beside the bed, flipped it…and saw a girl in camo, her dripping blond hair clinging to her cheek.

She'd been pinned by the prey she'd meant to hunt, and her cheeks were flushed with embarrassment, or maybe fear. Her jewellike and very un-Japanese eyes were slightly damp and wavering.

"You're…"

Then the girl told me who she was.

"It's me—Charlotte Arisaka Anderson."

◆ I can forgive everything but that triumphant look

"Charlie?"

I knew this girl.

Charlotte Arisaka Anderson.

She was sixteen, and although she was an American citizen, she had Japanese blood as well. She was an agent who flew all over the world on orders from the organization she belonged to, and on Siesta's request, she'd worked with us a few times—meaning she knew me, too.

"Are you okay?" I asked Charlie nervously.

"……Yes, mostly."

Holding her injured right shoulder, Charlie slowly sat up on the bed. I straightened up, too, stepping back.

What was she doing here, though? Why had she sneaked into my room with a weapon…?

"Oh, I see what's going on. Siesta asked you to do this, didn't she?"

Was this the "step" Siesta had said she'd taken? I see… Yes, with combat skills like Charlie's, we'd be able to fight the enemy on equal terms. Apparently, I'd jumped the gun, and now I was guilty of excessive self-defense.

"…She sure did. I swear… You just lunged at me out of nowhere."

"Look, I'm sorry, okay? But you did come in here with a gun."

"Well, Cerberus might have gotten in ahead of me."

I see. Yeah, that's true. I might have been a little too wary myself. A little more of that, and I would have had Siesta laughing at me for freaking out.

"Hmm. Something smells." Charlie sniffed audibly.

"Does it? Did you fart?"

"Are you familiar with the word *tact*?"

"Well, my ace detective partner sure isn't." I went over to the window to air out the room for Charlie.

"Still, you're better than I thought you were, Kimizuka. You completely crushed me," she said behind me. "Even if you did use a trick, I never thought you'd manage to pin me…"

"Yeah, I guess it really is the first time I've ever beaten you one-on-one."

That training Siesta puts me through all the time must be paying off, I thought. I set a hand on the curtain, and just as I opened the window—

"No, really, could I actually beat Charlie?"

It was a completely pathetic self-evaluation, a deduction with zero pride.

The thing is, though, I knew.

I knew how strong Charlotte Arisaka Anderson was. I also knew that Siesta was the first to acknowledge that strength. Charlotte would never lose to a guy like me.

"...Uh, more important."

I had a simpler theory, too.

"That short-tempered sore loser would never admit she lost this easily."

Especially not to me, her mortal enemy. Therefore—

"Who are you?"

I turned around, directing my question at Charlie...or more precisely, at the individual who was passing as Charlotte Arisaka Anderson.

"Ah—you've seen through my disguise, then?"

The voice shifted from Charlie's into a deep male voice. In the next moment, her face and body warped and changed into a sturdy middle-aged man in a black robe.

"Well, no matter. Either way, I shall take your heart."

"...! So you really are Cerberus?"

That ability to transform must be where he'd gotten his code name. The guard dog of Hades had three heads, a symbol of an ability to change into other people. If his nose was sharp, too, of course the police would have a hard time with him. No wonder they hadn't managed to catch him yet.

"Bad news, though. Your Jack the Ripper imitation ends today." I'd retrieved the Magnum during that fight, and I pointed it at his forehead.

"You do seem quite capable. I thought you were that ace detective's lackey, but I shall have to revise that impression."

As Cerberus spoke, he quietly closed his eyes and put his palms together in front of his chest. The gesture reminded me of a priest, although the impression was lessened somewhat by his pompous way of speaking and sturdy build. However, I was only able to think that for a moment, before—

"The moon is full tonight. It makes the blood sing."

The next moment, Cerberus's muscles began swelling up, and then thick fur spread over his body. He looked just like—

"Wait, you're a werewolf...?"

Aren't you confusing Cerberus with something else? But this wasn't really a situation for snappy comebacks.

"If you get shot, don't come crying to me."

I squeezed the trigger, firing bullets—but...

"Save those words until after you've hit me."

With truly beast-like agility, Cerberus evaded them.

"Ghk...!"

Once he'd dodged all my attacks, the huge creature lunged at me.

There were sharp claws right in front of my face, and I had no weapons.

Realizing I was a moment away from tragedy, I squeezed my eyes shut—

"Get down."

Hearing *the voice from the phone receiver*, at the last moment, I managed to drop into a crouch.

"—Khah, hah!"

The next thing I heard was a gunshot and a low groan. When I opened my eyes, the beast-man was lying there, dark blood streaming from his shoulder.

"...So opening the window saved my butt?"

Remembering that I'd never ended that call, I put my phone to my ear and spoke to her.

"Hey, why did you wait this long? You'd better not tell me you were sleeping."

At that...

"I did make it in time, so does it matter?"

By then, I was hearing the voice from the phone and right behind me.

Making the grumpiest face I could manage, I turned around—and there, standing on the sill of the large window and looking very pleased with herself, was a white-haired girl.

"Did you miss me?"

◆ The crimson devil, the ice queen

"Well, now," said Siesta.

She lunged at the fallen Cerberus, musket at the ready, then straddled him and jammed the muzzle against his skin.

"Hmm, déjà vu."

The scene from the plane, three years ago, flashed through my mind's eye. That time, too, Siesta had shoved her gun against Bat's head to get the hijacking under control like an action movie heroine.

"Why you…! When did you make your approach?" Cerberus growled from where she had him pinned; his expression was agonized. "My nose told me nothing of your presence…so why?"

Yes, that had been Siesta's plan: use me as a solitary decoy, while she lurked someplace beyond the range of Cerberus's nose… But then she had stepped onto the battlefield unnoticed.

"Apparently, there's still a little of that smell left." Siesta sniffed.

"It smells?"

"Huh? Didn't you notice before you opened the window, Kimi? Until a minute ago, this room was filled with a special type of gas."

"Gas? Oh, come to think of it…"

When Cerberus had still been disguised as Charlie, he'd been bothered by the smell in the room. It couldn't be… But when had it happened?

"Those." Siesta pointed up at the ceiling—or to be more precise…

"The sprinklers, huh?"

That was probably the real "step" that Siesta had taken. She'd seen that I was carrying a Zippo lighter around, predicted the possibility that the sprinklers would come on during this fight, and rigged up gas to apply along with the water. The gas had numbed Cerberus's superhuman nose, and he'd failed to notice Siesta.

"...As always, you're way too prepared."

It was as if Siesta had known everything that was going to happen before it happened.

"The upshot is, I win. Accept it."

Siesta shoved the muzzle of her gun at Cerberus again. Thinking I'd contact Ms. Fuubi while I had the chance, I took out my smartphone— and that's when it happened.

"I cannot allow myself to be apprehended yet."

No sooner had Cerberus spoken than his body *rapidly began to shrink.*

"—! His transformation ability!"

In a moment, Cerberus was as small as a child, and he slipped out of Siesta's hold.

"Assistant! Shut the window!"

We're not letting him get away...!

Hastily turning to the window behind me, I tried to cut off Cerberus's escape route, but...

"Too late."

By then, he'd already resumed his beast-man form and was leaping lightly over my head.

"I have a mission. One more. I must obtain just one more fresh heart, and until then..."

He leaned out the window, and—

"You can leave yours, Cerberus."

A spray of blood.

Then Cerberus's head—only his head—fell out of the window and down. After a moment, his decapitated body slowly toppled over backward.

"...Huh?"

My mind couldn't process what I was seeing. Why was Cerberus dead?

Who was it? Who'd done this?

"Assistant!" That was Siesta. She sounded more flustered and tense than I'd ever heard her. "Be careful."

She was pointing her musket at the window, but its muzzle seemed to be wavering slightly.

"This is the first time we've met in person, isn't it, ace detective," said a bitterly cold voice.

The speaker, who was sitting on the windowsill, swung the saber she'd used to cut down Cerberus, shaking off the blood.

"You're…"

A girl with short black hair and red eyes. She wore a wine-red military uniform, and multiple sabers hung from her waist. She seemed to be about Siesta's age. Between her service cap and her high collar, I couldn't make out her face all that well.

But the flawless ace detective was wary of her. Who in the world was—?

"My name—my code name—Is Hel," she droned from her perch in the window, cleaning the blood off her sword with a cloth.

"Code name… So she's another one?"

"She's one of SPES's highest-ranking officers," murmured Siesta. She was standing next to me now, and her expression was grim. "In Norse mythology, Hel is the name of the queen who ruled Niflheim, the country of ice."

"So there's no system to their code names, huh?"

At the very least, it was clear that she was in a different league from Bat and Cerberus.

"Well, now."

Hel descended from the windowsill and proceeded straight to Cerberus's corpse, without so much as a glance at us. She crouched down—and plunged her sword into the left side of his chest.

"…Ughk." The gruesome sight made me feel sick.

With a face that held no emotion, Hel stuck her arm into Cerberus's chest…then pulled something out of the pooled blood.

"Now we have the final piece." Hel's gory right hand held what looked like a small lump of black ore. "Now then, I'll take this back with me and commence the operation…"

"Do you think we'll let you?" Siesta glared sharply at Hel. The aim of the long-barreled gun was perfectly steady now.

"Well, well." Hel returned Siesta's gaze. "But *you cannot shoot.*"

"What are you talking ab…—?"

Abruptly, as if she'd noticed something, Siesta's eyebrows rose.

"And you cannot take a single step from that spot. You cannot speak."

Hel's bloodred eyes glinted ominously.

Siesta's eyes widened. Her mouth flapped as if she were a fish who'd poked her head out of the water in search of food, but she didn't say a word.

"It can't be— A pseudohuman ability…"

If Hel was also a member of SPES, then she would have had some sort of special power. If she could do this, was it an ability that controlled what others did…?

I was in too much of a panic to think through it rationally, though. She had Siesta nailed down. In that case, our enemy's next move was obvious.

The girl in the red military uniform sprinted toward me.

"Now, why don't you come see hell with me?"

In that moment, my mind lost its link to the world.

◆ Toward the future, one year from now

"Where…?"

When I opened my eyes, my surroundings were dark and unfamiliar.

"……!"

My arms were handcuffed, and my legs were chained. The legs of the chair they'd put me in seemed to be bolted to the concrete floor, and the smell of mold stung my nostrils. My voice was echoing, too… Was I underground?

"It looks like you're awake."

A figure emerged from the darkness.

She wore a service cap, pulled down low, and a red military uniform with a stand-up collar. I could barely see her expression, but there was no mistaking her. It was the girl who'd abducted me and brought me here—

"Hel!"

I'd met her at that hotel, and then…

"Where is this place? Are you planning to…kill me?"

I gulped. Why had she gone to the trouble of separating me from Siesta then bringing me all the way here?

"Would you join us?"

I hadn't been expecting that at all, and for a moment, my mind went blank.

"What are you saying?"

The next thing I knew, Hel was behind me.

"Yes, that was a bit misleading, wasn't it? —I want you to be my partner."

The voice made me imagine her tongue on my ear, and goose bumps broke out all across my skin.

"...I don't get it. What would you get out of having me as a partner?"

"You don't think much of yourself, do you?"

"I prefer to call it *modesty*."

Even at a time like this, the nonsense just came naturally. In fact, maybe it was *because* I was in so much danger. If I didn't have my snark, I'd have a hard time hanging on to my sanity. This girl, Hel, was menacing enough to make me shudder.

"No, don't misunderstand. This is the shaking of a warrior."

"I didn't say anything."

"If you think I wet my pants, you're free to check."

"I see. So *you two* joke around like that all the time." Hel smiled thinly, then finally stepped away from my back.

"...Didn't know you knew how to smile."

"Ah-ha-ha. That's a mean thing to say. What do you think I am?" Footsteps clicking against the floor, Hel walked around my chair in a wide circle. "A devil without emotions? A monster who doesn't speak your language? A villain you could never reach an understanding with? You really are unkind." Hel gave another thin smile. "After all, I'm *just a girl*."

Hel crossed in front of me. She was holding a thick volume she'd picked up somewhere, her eyes on its pages.

"I really doubt 'just a girl' could kill a comrade in cold blood," I retorted, remembering what Hel had done to Cerberus at the hotel.

"Comrade? Ah-ha-ha, no, no. That was nothing more than a *component*, there to carry the plan to a successful conclusion." Hel laughed aloud, as if I'd told a really funny joke. The sound was carefree, easygoing, artless— and cruel. Just like Hel herself, it seemed.

"Are you planning to use me and throw me away, too? Plus, you've got nothing to gain by making me your partner."

I couldn't believe that was what she genuinely wanted. What was she plotting?

"You're asking what's in it for me?" Hel looked down at the book. "Before any talk of pros and cons, what's written in the sacred text is absolute, you know."

"The sacred text?"

Did she mean the book she was holding?

"What I have here is only a portion of it. Several things that will happen to you in the future are written in it."

"That's just crazy—"

"—And it couldn't possibly happen? And yet they have. For example, this sacred text definitely predicted that Cerberus would die there, and you would come here."

That had to be a lie. She was just talking about things that had already happened as if they'd been prophesied long ago.

"You don't look as if you believe me."

"Yeah, but don't take it too hard. I don't believe anyone but myself."

"What a coincidence. I'm the same way."

We might be able to get along pretty well, then. Not that I want to.

"In that case, have you heard of the Leaves of Agastya?" Hel asked. The open book was still in her hands.

"The Leaves of Agastya... I'm pretty sure it was a book of prophecies written by an Indian holy man, a few thousand years ago..."

Siesta was always telling me miscellaneous information and trivia, and I got the feeling she had mentioned this to me. Long ago, the Indian sage Agastya had written revelations he'd received from the gods on palm leaves in ancient Tamil, or something to that effect. She'd also said that each person's future had been laid out in detail.

"This sacred text was created with the Leaves of Agastya as its foundation. Your future is written here as well." With her eyes on the open book, Hel walked around the spacious room. "For example, about one month from now, you'll go back to that normal routine you've always longed for and live as an ordinary high schooler."

"Not a chance. That ace detective would never let me go so easily."

Of course, if she meant we'd completely destroy SPES a month from now, get our happy ending, and then go back to our normal routines, I'd welcome it, but…

"One year later, you will take up the mantle again, in a role that is closer to 'detective' than 'assistant,' and play an important role in resolving multiple cases."

"That's not happening, either. I've never been anything other than Siesta's assistant."

After all, there's no way she'd yield her cushy position as the detective to me, is there?

"A heart's forgotten memories, a miraculous sapphire worth three billion yen, and the legacy left by the ace detective. If you happen to remember these words a year from now, you'll be able to verify the answers for yourself."

"Look, what is this about? What are you saying?"

"What was it—your knack for being dragged into things?"

Hel closed the book. I hadn't told her about that. She couldn't be implying that the Leaves of Agastya had covered that, too, could she?

"I don't think that's quite it, though."

"…What are you talking about?"

"You don't get dragged into things. You drag others in. You drag the whole world in," Hel said, pointedly spreading her arms wide. "That knack of yours is the power to transform everything and trigger incidents. You yourself are the center of the world. I'll make you my partner so that you can save it alongside me."

"I think you meant 'destroy it.'"

"As far as I'm concerned, they're one and the same."

"You're telling me that destroying the world will get you something you want?"

"You could say that."

"What if I refuse?"

"Then you refuse." Hel spun around and started to walk away.

"According to the sacred text, you won't be mine for a while yet. It's only that getting things done ahead of schedule would make Father—" She suddenly snapped her mouth shut.

Father? Who was that?

"It's too bad, though. Being my partner would come with a variety of perks," she went on. She was taking on a joking tone, as if she'd never made that earlier remark. "First and most important, you'd be paid for doing nothing."

"Hell of a bargain to start with."

I'd love for a certain ace detective who insists on working me like a dog to hear that.

"You can play video games on a big-screen TV from morning to night if you want."

"Are you an angel?"

"You can have snacks and ice cream and cup ramen whenever you like, as much as you like."

"Are you a goddess?"

Hey, white-haired ace detective, did you hear that? A villain is promising to be my sugar mama. You've got two seconds before I flip.

"So what do you say?"

The girl in the military uniform held her right hand out to me, where I sat in the chair.

"Kimi— Be my partner."

With an artless smile, she made me a very attractive offer.

And my response was:

"Yeah—of course not."

Sorry about that. I've always been a coward, and I base my decisions on what I have to lose, not what I have to gain.

"After all, I'd be more scared to make an enemy of Siesta than of you." Smiling a little at the ironic choice I'd been given, I turned Hel's proposal down point-blank. "You didn't even think I'd take your hand, did you?"

"Ah-ha-ha. You knew?" Hel grinned like a little kid whose prank had been discovered, turned, and walked away. While she had her back to me, I tried to figure out a way to get the handcuffs off.

Honestly, I'm impressed she had the nerve to extend her hand to me, when she was the reason I literally couldn't take it. She'd assumed all along that I was going to turn her down.

"In exchange, then, there's a little something I'd like you to watch."

The next moment, the room got a bit brighter. *Hel must have flipped a light switch or something.* I looked around, and—

"What...the hell...?"

For as far as I could see, there was *something,* hidden in the shadows.

It was in an iron cage, and it reminded me of an enormous reptile. However, I'd never actually seen a creature like it before. The closest thing I could think of was that *Alien* monster I'd seen in some movie a while back.

It looked close to four meters long. I didn't see anything resembling eyes in its head, and fangs sprouted from its enormous jaw. A viscous liquid dribbled from its mouth at regular intervals, and while I did see minimal signs of life, it was very still. Asleep, maybe?

"It's a biological weapon," Hel told me, indifferently. "Its breath holds a toxin that readily binds with atmospheric oxygen."

"...So you're going to use that thing in a terrorist attack? Here in London?"

"Exactly. That's the history of the future, recorded in the sacred text. It's God's salvation."

"In what religion...?"

Rgh, pseudohumans hadn't been enough for them? They'd had to make a thing like this? If they let this monster loose in a populated area... Actually, that reminds me—where were we now? Where was she planning to unleash that monster? We didn't seem to have left London, but...

"Oh, come to think of it, you asked where we were. I haven't told you yet."

Hel put a hand into the iron cage, caressing the biological weapon's head affectionately.

"We're under the building where the British houses of Parliament meet: the Palace of Westminster."

◆ It's way too late to act cool

"...If you have a facility like this directly under the nerve center of the country, it seems safe to assume you've got a significant number of collaborators."

For the past three years, Siesta and I had been fighting SPES constantly, and yet we hadn't been able to completely stop their invasion. It had already progressed far beyond what we'd imagined.

"It's just as you say. We have comrades all over the world, in politics, finance, the police, the clergy... It's quite possible that someone right next to you is actually a member of SPES."

"That's one hell of a punchline," I snapped.

While Hel's attention was on the biological weapon, I used my teeth to take out the wire I always keep in my breast pocket. I pushed it into the lock on my handcuffs, then twisted it around at random, relying on instinct and long years of experience. I don't say I've got a knack for getting dragged into trouble for nothing. I'm used to getting kidnapped and locked up.

"Why would you tell me about that plot, though?" I stayed in the conversation, participating enough to keep her from getting suspicious. "What's the point of showing me that monster? Are you planning to make me its first meal?"

"Its meal, hmm?" Hel said.

From behind her, I saw her stop moving.

"...Well, uh, just as a figure of speech."

I should not have said that. Whatever else they do to me, don't let me get eaten by that disgusting thing...

"You're on the right track, although you guessed wrong."

...That was close. I'd had an actual brush with death there.

Still, that "right track" Hel had mentioned was concerning. It couldn't be—

"Are you planning to release that thing into the city and let it eat people?"

"Oh, no, no. We've already given it plenty to eat."

"You have? ...—!"

Was that what was going on...? The heart-hunt that had broken out lately, courtesy of Cerberus, centered on London. The true reason for those incidents had been—

"That monster *eats human hearts?*"

That was its food, or possibly its source of power. The biological weapon ran on human flesh and blood.

"Impressive. You really do have good instincts. I knew you'd be a fitting partner for me."

"—I told you I want none of that."

Finally, the handcuffs came off, and I quickly freed my legs. I'd heard wind; I started to cut and run toward the source of the sound—

"Where are you planning to go?"

She was onto me instantly. Well, if I'd run off, she would only have caught me anyway.

"You will be my partner someday, and I want you to watch what's about to happen, no matter what. Come, Betelgeuse." I assume that was the weapon's name.

Hel took something from the sleeve of her military uniform.

"That black rock…"

I was pretty sure it was the object Hel had pulled out of Cerberus's chest cavity. If human hearts were this living weapon's energy source, this was probably the final key that would activate it.

"Betelgeuse, it's time to go to work."

With that, Hel pushed the small stone into the left side of the biological weapon's chest. And then…

"—grr, —guh, —!, ——ghkgyaaaaaah!"

A roar reverberated down the underground road. The bioweapon was awake.

As if its restraints had suddenly broken, the enormous monster thrashed its whole body against the metal cage, venting its agitation. Then—

"Aaaaaaaaaaaaaaaaaaaaaaaaaaaaah!"

In no time at all, with a ferocious crash, it burst out of the cage. Unable to control itself, the monster lunged at Hel, as if it meant to swallow her whole.

"Goodness, you're noisy." Hel's red eyes pierced the monster. In the next instant…

"—! Gyaaaaaaaaaaaaaaaaah!"

In motions too fast for my eyes to follow, Hel drew several sabers, then plunged them into Betelgeuse, all over its body.

"Settle down a little, all right?"

Betelgeuse suddenly turned meek, crouching down like a giant pet.

"You're planning to let a monster like that loose? ...You're insane."

"It's destiny. It's my mission."

"In that case, this ends here and now."

"Oh, really? You're going to stop me on your own?" Hel's painted lips curved.

"That's a great smile."

"Hmm? Are you hitting on me?"

"I'm being diplomatic. Sorry, but there's no way I'll ever be your partner."

After that last casual exchange, we were both certain we'd be parting ways.

"I see. That's a pity. For now, then, watch this city crumble." Hel leaped onto Betelgeuse, straddling its neck. She was probably planning to head aboveground, then start by crushing the nerve center of the country.

However, I'd already told her. "This ends now."

"How, exactly? You don't even have a weapon, so how on earth..."

"You've got the wrong idea. *When did I ever say I'd be the one to stop you?*"

Come on. You know there's no way she'd let me steal the show.

"—Assistant!"

Like a ray of light in the darkness, a warm voice filtered in to us from elsewhere in the facility.

"Assistant... Where are you?!"

It came closer and closer, until we were hearing it loud and clear from the left-hand wall.

"Assistant...! Where is my assistant?! Assistant!"

...Yeah, you don't have to yell it over and over like that. Calm down. I'm right here.

"Hello?! Assistant... He's not here... Where is he?! Where is my assistant?! Assistant... I can't find— Assistant...!"

Um... No. This is, uh... Is she okay?

Facing each other after this was going to be really awkward, wasn't it?

"...! Argh, this wall! It's in the way! I don't need this right now! Ugh, just break already! Get out of my way!"

The next moment, there was an earsplitting crash, and—

"Assistant!"

Siesta, piloting a giant robot, smashed through the wall. Part of the cockpit was transparent, and her expression was more anxious and panicked than I'd ever seen it. The pale silver hair she was so proud of was completely disheveled.

However, although Siesta was panting heavily, it didn't take her long to notice me and assess that I was fine. We gazed at each other for a full ten seconds, and then—

"Whew. I swear, Assistant, you're an awful lot of trouble."

"You missed your chance to act cool a while back."

◆ You're an angel, I'm a monster

Once again, I turned my attention to the humanoid combat weapon that Siesta had arrived in.

Its armored shape was mostly white and about five meters tall— slightly larger than Hel's biological weapon. An area near the head of the unit was glass, and I could see Siesta sitting inside. That was probably the cockpit.

The machine could have stepped straight out of a robot anime. Its thick arms and legs were striking, but I spotted missile and bullet firing ports at its joints. It really was a combat weapon.

...Which was why a question came to mind. "Siesta, where did you get that thing?"

It probably hadn't been more than a few hours since I'd been abducted.

How had she managed to procure a mobile weapon in that brief time frame?

In response to my perfectly natural question, Siesta said:

"...Um, well, I found it...lying on the road?"

She was refusing to look at me.

"You are such a liar! You couldn't have just *found* that thing by the road!"

"...No, I mean it. What, you think I was so shaken by your abduction that I freaked out, negotiated with the British government, and borrowed the experimental military weapon Sirius? No way."

"That was even more elaborate than I expected!"

She just spilled all of it herself. She's so bad at lying, it's unreal.

"Siesta, look, you were way too desperate to save me."

"...! ...I'm telling you, that wasn't it!" Siesta murmured. She had turned her face away, and I couldn't see it clearly.

"Honestly. You'll make me jealous, having such a passionate exchange with my future partner," Hel remarked, without a hint of jealousy or even interest.

"Hel."

Siesta's blue eyes glared at Hel from the cockpit.

Hel responded by preparing for battle, straddling Betelgeuse's neck as it leaned forward.

"I won't let you have your way with this city anymore."

"Do you seriously think you can stop me? Do you think you can stop destiny?"

And with that, the battle was on.

"—Ghkgyaaaaaaaaah!" The monster roared and lunged toward us on all fours.

"Assistant!"

Opening the hatch and leaning halfway out of the pilot's seat, Siesta reached for me. I grabbed her hand, let her pull me up, and slid into the unit.

"...This is cramped."

"Well, it was built for one, you know."

Pressed together in the tight cockpit, Siesta and I headed into battle with the monster.

"I'll control the right side, so you work the left side, Kimi."

"Don't just make me pilot this thing out of nowhere. I don't even have a regular driver's license."

"Well, desperate times. I can't reach over there with you in the way. Hurry up, here it comes."

Betelgeuse and Hel hadn't wasted any time; they were leaping at us from the left.

"...—! Okay, fine!"

This was no time to hesitate. I grabbed a lever on instinct, attempting to steer the unit...but—

"Whoaaaaa?!"

The Sirius, with us in it, promptly lost its balance and fell over.

"Ow-ow-ow... What is this for, the leg?"

Dammit. That was supposed to be an epic rocket punch.

However, we were still okay. When its target had suddenly disappeared, Betelgeuse had overshot, tumbling behind us. We were fighting a monster that had just woken up. It had power, but not control. We were probably pretty evenly matched.

"If you've got time to analyze the situation, could you use it to get off me?"

"Hmm? ......Oh."

I'd fallen over, and Siesta's cold, irritated eyes were right below me. Apparently, my hand had landed somewhere unfortunate, and I hastily pulled away. Although the cockpit was so small that there wasn't much distance to take.

"All right, this isn't going to work. I suppose I'll do the piloting after all."

"But you can't reach the levers if we're sitting side-by-side, right?"

"Not if we're sitting side-by-side, no."

...Oh. Well, I guess it's our only option.

"—Ghkgyaaaaaaaaaaaaaaaaaah!"

Behind us, the living weapon was roaring. We hastily got ourselves into position, worked the levers, and got the fallen unit back on its feet.

"If you take advantage of this situation to touch me somewhere you shouldn't, I'll lose all respect for you."

"Zero trust for your assistant, huh?" I sighed, fastening the seatbelt.

"I'm joking. All right, here we go for real this time— Sirius, move out."

At that, Siesta gripped the control stick firmly from *where she was sitting on my lap*.

"Here we go."

"Whoa…!"

With a roar from the engine, the unit surged forward, straight toward the grotesque, four-legged monster. With that much propulsion, we closed the distance in no time.

"Let's go for the direct approach."

Hel was right in front of us, on Betelgeuse's neck. With a violent crash, the humanoid weapon and the biological weapon locked together.

"I can't believe you'd create a monster like that."

As Siesta pushed the steering lever forward, she glared through the glass at Hel, astride the monster.

"You're very much in the way." Hel turned her cold red eyes on Siesta. The easy indifference she'd had during our conversation had been replaced by open hostility.

"That's my mission," Siesta said and set her fingertip on a button. A spot near the Sirius's wrist fired a stream of bullets.

"——!"

When Hel saw it, she lightly jabbed Betelgeuse's back with a saber, using the pain to control its movements, and dodged our attack. She reminded me of a jockey expertly controlling her horse with a whip.

But Hel didn't seem to like her chances against us in a straight fight, so she ignored us and drove Betelgeuse up the underground road.

"Siesta, don't let her get away! Her only goal is to unleash that monster on this city!"

As far as Hel was concerned, she didn't necessarily have to fight us. The houses of the British Parliament met right above this underground road. All she had to do was hit them, and the damage would be immeasurable.

"I know. Don't start with exposition just because you don't have anything to do."

"Geez, you're so unfair..."

Shoving the control stick forward, Siesta went after Hel and Betelgeuse. "My, you're stubborn."

As we caught up again, Hel drew one of her many sabers from her waist and flung it at us.

"......!"

Undaunted, Siesta tried to intercept it with the unit's machine gun—but even if our power was unmistakably greater, the monster had the upper hand in terms of mobility. It evaded all our bullets; all we hit was empty space.

"Hel... Why would you carry out a terror attack like this?"

As Siesta searched for a chance to win, she kept racing down the subterranean tunnel beside the enemy.

"Why? Because it's destiny." From her position astride Betelgeuse, Hel glanced over at us. "My will has nothing to do with it. I'm only following the sacred text."

"—Yeah, and you've been talking about nothing else this entire time."

It was so impossible to get through to her that I was getting pissed off.

At least Siesta seemed to feel the same way.

"No, I'm asking about *you*. What exactly are *you* thinking in all this?"

The Sirius's right arm took a swing at Betelgeuse...but as before, the monster nimbly evaded.

"Me? As I said, my intention is to bring about the future written in this sacred text. That is my only reason for existing. The only reason I was born."

Hel stuck a sword into Betelgeuse's back. With a little groan, the monster sped up, fleeing along the wall.

"Siesta!"

"It's all right, I won't let them get away. Hold on tight."

"Yeah, I'm counting on you!"

"I told you to hold on, but I didn't expect you to hug me quite so hard."

Well, there wasn't anything else to hold on to. I didn't have much choice.

Flames from the engine roared out of the Sirius's legs, and once again, we closed the distance to Betelgeuse in a rush.

"Earlier, you said that your mission was to get in our way, didn't you?" Hel said, once we'd caught up to her again. She glanced at us out of the corner of her eye.

"In that case, why are you a detective? Why do you protect people? Because that's what you were born to be, nothing more. I'm the same. Just as you were born to protect the world, I was born to destroy it. I came into the world bearing that role. Do you think I crave power? Destruction? I want none of those things. I'm merely obeying my natural instincts."

In the next instant, Betelgeuse abruptly switched direction, clamping its jaws around the Sirius's throat. Its fangs sank into the armor, and a worrying metallic noise echoed in the tunnel.

"...! So you're saying we're essentially the same? That there isn't even a moral difference between us?"

Siesta fought back in the Sirius, slamming Betelgeuse into the walls and floor, over and over. The humanoid and biological weapons attacked each other again and again, jostling as they made their way toward the underground road's exit.

"There may be a moral difference. I don't mind if there is."

Hel jammed sabers into the Sirius's knee joints. The unit tottered, and Betelgeuse seized the opportunity to *climb*. That proved we were near the exit to the surface...and Parliament. We weren't going to be able to stop the monster while it was still underground...

"Siesta!"

"Engine at full throttle."

I reached in from behind Siesta, setting my hands over hers, and we pushed the control stick forward. Large, mechanical wings sprouted from the Sirius's back, the engine roared, and we rose into the air.

In the time it took us to get airborne, the ceiling of the underground facility had opened to reveal black space above us.

"You are good, and I'm evil. That's fine." Hel and Betelgeuse flew up into the outside world.

"Wait...!"

We launched ourselves as well, chasing after them in the Sirius.

The moon and countless stars shone in the dark sky. Betelgeuse was climbing up Big Ben, the enormous clock tower attached to Westminster Palace.

"You are an angel; I am a monster. That's fine. It's what I've always wanted."

Before long, Hel and Betelgeuse alighted on the top of the tower.

The bioweapon's mouth opened; that poisonous breath would bring death to anything living and cause a massive tragedy. SPES's terror attack would be complete.

But we could still catch up.

Just a little farther; one more step.

If we could only reach it…

"Assistant," Siesta called to me without turning around. "You need to get away from this place quickly. No matter what happens."

…What was she saying?

But by the time I tried to ask, I'd already been flung out of the hatch into empty space.

The world flipped end over end. Was I spinning, or was it everything else? My sense of direction was completely scrambled—but before long, something yanked on my back, and the next thing I knew, I was drifting in the night sky with the help of a parachute.

"Siesta, why…?"

In the next instant—

At the top of the tower looming against the darkness, I saw the monster and robot clash—and then they both plunged toward the ground.

◆ Thank you for getting mad

"Siesta!"

A great column of flame rose in the dark streets.

That was where the Sirius and Betelgeuse had landed, meaning their pilots also had to be there. As sirens wailed in the distance, I made it to ground zero a slight distance away.

"Siesta… Hey, Siesta! Where are you, where did you go? …Siesta!"

Between the smoke and the hot wind, I couldn't keep my eyes open. A nasty, scorched smell was making my head swim; my whole body was hot, and my knees were ready to give out at any moment. I stumbled forward through it, shielding my face with my arms, and then—

"...Are you stupid, Kimi?"

My ears caught a warm voice I could never mistake for anyone else's, even in the middle of the burning wreckage.

"You're hardly qualified to talk about other people. You don't have to call me over and over like that; I can hear you."

The wind blew, and the smoke cleared slightly to reveal Siesta.

Her fair skin was smudged with soot, and she was bleeding so much that just seeing her brought me pain.

"You're the one who's stupid." I ran up to her and pulled her petite body into a hug before I knew what I was doing. "Why would you do something that reckless? Why did you send me away by myself?"

Siesta had probably been planning to evacuate me on my own all along. That unit was built for one, and it had only one ejection device. Back when she had me sit in that seat, this was the plan.

"...Only as a last resort. I had no intention of dying here, personally. However, if only one of us could survive, I—"

"Like hell!"

The angry yell came from way down in the pit of my stomach, and Siesta's blue eyes widened.

Good. Widen your ears, too, and listen reeeeeally carefully.

"Don't go talking like some philosopher, okay? Look. Three years ago, on that plane, ten thousand meters up, you recruited me. You made that choice; you'd damn well better look after me until the very...very, very end. Listen, I'm sorry, but I know I can never really get away from SPES without you. I'd die without you, all right?! If you understand that, then do your damn job and *keep me safe*, goddammit!"

My body was hot.

Was it because there was a column of fire beside me?

Or was it because I'd been shouting with everything I had?

No, it was because I'd been yelling at her for the most pathetic reason:

You have to stay alive so you can protect me. My breath came out ragged as I exhaled, and I was gushing sweat from every pore.

"…No one's ever scolded me so much in my entire life." Siesta stared up at me, a bit dazed. "I didn't know you could get so angry. How do I put this—"

"Surprised?"

"Amused."

"Oh, come on."

Look, I told you, don't laugh at me.

"Heh-heh." True to her words, Siesta let a giggle slip. "You'd die without me, hmm?"

"Hey, don't take that out of context."

"That was quite an impassioned proposal."

"I'm not proposing!"

"Well, try again after you turn eighteen."

"I told you—! Haaah, never mind…"

"Heh-heh!" Every so often, that cool mask would crack, and she'd laugh without a care in the world.

Sheesh, this ace detective…

"I promise you this."

Siesta glanced up, smoothly.

"I won't go off and die without telling you. —I swear I won't. Thanks for yelling at me."

With a light thump, Siesta let her forehead rest against my chest.

That was when it happened.

"——! Oww—!"

Something grazed my left eye. My vision went red… Had blood gotten in my eye? What was that? What had flown at me?!

"Assistant!" Siesta's eyes were wide and worried. *Yeesh, that expression doesn't suit you at all.*

"I'm fine. More important…"

I directed Siesta's attention straight ahead, to…

"Hff… Hff, not yet. I can't…die yet… Not here…"

From beyond the blazing flames, hell itself was bearing down on us, wrapped in black smoke.

"Hel…"

She was back. And she was even more torn up than Siesta was, holding only one red sword.

"You're alive." Siesta took a step forward, shielding me.

"Of…course. I'm not…destined…to die…here."

She wasn't holding the sacred text anymore; it must have burned up in the explosion. Even so, as if she was still trying to keep the promise, Hel mimed opening it.

"I'm the one who'll win in the end. If not, *giving this to Father will have been meaningless…!*"

For the first time, Hel showed something resembling real emotion.

"I see. You're…"

Siesta's blue eyes widened in surprise.

"Siesta?"

Hey. What did you just realize?

"Now…I can…end this."

But before I could actually ask the question, Hel leveled her military sword.

"*You will be unable to move a step from that spot, and my sword will run you through!*"

Her red eyes flashed the color of blood, and she charged at Siesta, who stood frozen.

"Siesta, run!" I yelled without thinking…but Siesta didn't budge. It was as if her feet had been glued to the asphalt. "Hel's ability…!"

It was mind control, or something like it. When those red eyes turned their gaze on you, you were possessed by the compulsion to do whatever Hel told you. Siesta had already fallen under their spell, and now she couldn't move…!

"Siesta!"

The tip of Hel's saber relentlessly rushed toward Siesta, and then—

"…………Huh?"

Hel gasped.

Her red eyes wandered, wavering. Then she looked down at herself.

Hel had thrust the crimson blade through her own chest.

"Wh... Why...?"

The next thing her dumbstruck eyes saw was the hand mirror Siesta wore at her waist, attached to a chain.

Hel had been looking into her own red eyes as she said the words "My sword will run you through."

"Checkmate," said Siesta.

Hel crumpled to the ground at her feet. "———!"

Blood was dripping slowly from somewhere near her heart. Her eyes were filled with confusion.

"How could I lose...? This...wasn't supposed to... I have...a mission... I have a mission, and I fight... ...Mission? Why was... Why was I...born? Why did I..."

"The answer..."

Siesta pulled the sword from Hel's chest, drawing a shriek and a spurt of blood from the girl.

"The answer will be waiting for you in hell."

Then Siesta swung the blade down at her enemy's drooping head.

But it wasn't over.

"—Chameleon...!"

Hel howled at the sky.

"! Is she signaling for some kind of attack?!"

Hastily, I scanned the area...but a moment later, I knew I'd guessed wrong.

"...! Her body's...disappeari..."

Not Siesta's—Hel's body had begun to vanish, melting little by little into the darkness as if she were being hidden by a transparent cloak.

"I won't let you get away!"

Leveling her musket, Siesta fired at the spot where Hel had been...but by then, there wasn't a trace of the enemy left.

"Siesta, is that Hel's ability, too?"

"No, probably not. It was one of her comrades," Siesta coolly explained and lowered her gun.

"Chameleon... That's a SPES code name, huh?"

With their ability, they could probably make themselves and whatever they touched vanish. If so, we couldn't go after Hel.

Just when we'd almost won, our worst enemy had slipped back into the darkness.

"So this was a draw, and everyone took damage?"

"Yes. Once we get home, we'll have to discuss our next steps."

Right. Hel was still alive somewhere. But she was also injured, which meant this could be our best chance. We needed to regroup, then go after her as soon as possible. Since we were in agreement on that, we were about to return to the hotel where we'd been earlier, when—

"———!"

Siesta took a step, and her face twisted.

"Siesta?"

"...Sorry."

As the word left her mouth, her knees buckled, and she collapsed.

◆ I'll forgive everything but that misunderstanding

"Aaaah."

The open mouth looked like it belonged to a baby bird waiting for food, and I held out a slice of the apple I'd peeled.

"...Nom... Mm...gulp... Hmm. This apple isn't very juicy."

"Don't complain when somebody's feeding you."

"Well, that's not my fault. I'm injured."

"Yeah—in your legs! Your hands are fine!"

In a room of our office-slash-living-space...

Siesta, who was laid up in bed, didn't flinch at my retort. Instead, she stretched flamboyantly. Rarely for her, she was wearing a hoodie along with other extremely casual clothes. However, there was a reason for her non-combat fashion choices.

"Did you already forget how you lectured an injured detective for ages?"

"...You acted like you were fine, so I thought it wasn't serious. Sorry."

"Well, I was also running on adrenaline, and I'd forgotten I was hurt."

"Then why am I the only one getting blamed?"

During that near-deadly fight at Big Ben a few days back, Siesta's legs had sustained injuries that would take two weeks to fully heal.

Hel had escaped, and by rights, we should have gone after her as quickly as possible. With Siesta laid up, though, that wasn't happening. We'd decided to base ourselves in London again and wait until she was all healed.

"Are you all right, Kimi?"

"Enough to bust my butt taking care of my selfish, demanding partner."

"I see. Good."

"That was sarcastic, you know. Extremely sarcastic. Don't ignore it."

"After all, if anything happened to you, I couldn't go on."

"...Where did the sappy stuff come from? Now you're just making it weird."

Plus, I highly doubt she's thinking anything that noble.

"Never mind, just hurry up and get yourself healed. I suck at housework."

I'd been traveling with Siesta for close to three years, and there had been quite a few times when we'd spent long stretches together under the same roof like this, but I'd left all the chores to her. I do feel bad about that, but it's a question of appropriate division of labor. Since she works me like a dog most of the time, I'd like to beg for a break of some kind, at least.

"It's cohabitation, the lifestyle you've always dreamed of. You could enjoy it just a little, couldn't you?"

"Don't call it cohabitation. We're strategic roommates."

"Besides, you should work on your ability to live independently. What are you going to do if I'm not around anymore?"

"...Hey. We're not talking about that."

"Oh, that's right."

"Don't want to get in trouble again," Siesta said with a little smile. "I would at least like you to learn to do laundry, though. Nobody likes grubby guys."

"I'd really love to accommodate you there, but... Well, you know. There are some, um…"

"Hmm? Oh, my undies?"

Hey, I was trying to be tactful. Don't just say it.

"If you're going to wear them on your head, do it where I can't see you," she said.

"That thought has literally never crossed my mind."

"Oh—well, if you're a sniffer, I'd really rather you didn't—"

"Like I said, don't you have any faith in your assistant?"

Seriously, what were these past three years, anyway?

"…Haah."

I swear, this partner of mine. I couldn't even crack a wry smile as I unsteadily got to my feet.

"Hmm? You're going out?"

"Huh? Yeah, to the supermarket."

"? Didn't you say you'd stocked up on everything we needed this morning?"

Hey, Siesta, come on. Get it together.

"You wanted *sweeter, juicier ones*, right?"

Sheesh. You literally just said it; I can't believe you forgot.

At that, Siesta stared blankly back at me for a few seconds—then dissolved into laughter.

"Wh-what? What's so funny?"

When Siesta laughed that way, she was always teasing me. But I couldn't think of any reason… What the heck had Siesta in stitches this time?

"…—, Kimi."

Fighting back laughter, Siesta finally managed to speak.

"I suspect you like me far too much."

……?! ……??!?!?!?!?!!

"Huh? You're not making any sense. Huh? No, huh? The hell??????"

What was she even talking about? Were her injuries getting to her? Was that why? Had she hit her head, too? She never would have said anything so ludicrous otherwise. I mean, come on. I was looking after a sick person. She said she wanted sweet apples, so I was just going to go buy some,

that's all... Or, I mean, okay, maybe it could seem a little like I was pampering her, or treasuring her too much, but that does *not* mean I think of Siesta as anybody special, and that misunderstanding is incredibly irritating, so yeah, basically—

"Shaddup, stupid!"

I got the feeling I was acting like a grade-schooler, but whatever. I needed to go outside and cool my head.

Hmm? Weird. For some reason, the doorknob slipped, and I couldn't seem to turn it.

Was it out of order? Yeah. Probably. Definitely. I kicked the door open and left the room.

"Dammit, I'm never coddling her again."

...Well, after this time. After all, she's injured. Yeah, just this once. This is a one-time-only deal. Telling myself that, I headed for the supermarket.

And on that shopping trip, in a back alley near the major thoroughfare known as Baker Street—I picked up a lost girl.

Interlude 2

"All right. I think I'll pause the film here for a moment."

The picture cut out, and Siesta appeared again.

"...Uh, that one really felt like you were trying to embarrass me, too."

Natsunagi, who was next to me, shot me a cold glance. *Don't look at me; I'm not responsible for any of this, all right?*

"They were always like that, Ma'am and Kimizuka," said Charlie. "Isn't it infuriating? Especially Kimizuka."

"It certainly is," Natsunagi agreed. "I think we can afford to bully him a bit. It's Kimizuka, after all."

"Why are you two bonding over this? I didn't think you got along."

If I remembered right, they'd fought plenty on that ship after they met for the first time.

"Mm, yes, what doesn't kill you makes you stronger," Saikawa offered sagely, although I had no idea what she was trying to say.

Well, if it brought those two closer together, I supposed I'd just have to take a little undeserved blame... Did I, though?

Agh. Anyway.

"...Hel, huh?"

She was the greatest enemy we'd encountered on that three-year journey. However, as that video had shown, Hel had summoned Chameleon and vanished into the darkness.

"I never dreamed someone had disguised himself as me. That's disgusting." Charlie scowled.

Yeah, I'd come pretty close to falling for Cerberus's disguise myself back then.

"Does that mean there might be a wolf here, pretending to be one of us?" Saikawa asked.

It scared me more than I'd expected. "Playing Werewolf with four people would be pretty tough. I doubt we'd be able to really get into it."

Which was why I cracked a joke to hide it.

"If there is a wolf here…there's only one I can think of," Natsunagi said. She was staring at me, unimpressed.

"True," said Charlie.

"Yes," said Saikawa. "You're right."

"Don't go agreeing with her. And don't try to ruin my reputation."

Even as we joked around with each other, though, there was something in that previous clip that I couldn't get out of my mind. It was what Hel had said to me when she'd abducted me.

"For example, about one month from now, you'll go back to that normal routine you've always longed for and live as an ordinary high schooler."

"Then, one year later, you will be placed in a role that is closer to 'detective' than 'assistant,' and will steer a variety of issues to their resolutions."

"A heart's forgotten memories, a miraculous sapphire with a market value of three billion yen, and the legacy left by the ace detective— If you happen to remember these words a year from now, you'll be able to verify the answers."

A year ago, I hadn't paid any attention to any of that. A "sacred text" that told the future? No one would believe that garbage. As a matter of fact, until I saw this footage, I'd completely forgotten about it.

But now that I'd heard those words again, they described my recent situation perfectly. Did that mean this future had already been predicted a year ago? In that case, what about the other thing Hel had said? The one about how I'd be her partner someday… Could that come true as well?

No, of course not. After all, while it hadn't come up in the video yet, ultimately, Hel had—

"Now then, shall we move on to the next clip?" Siesta interjected, and the picture on the screen changed again.

I was just discovering a girl sleeping in a cardboard box in one of London's back alleys.

"I won't stop the film again. Now then, watch for yourselves. See how I—and *those girls*—met our ends."

Chapter 3

◆ I pick up a little girl. Then I get fired.

In a narrow lane with no foot traffic, a girl was asleep in a cardboard box someone had thrown away.

Usually, it would be a kitten or a puppy, but this was a girl. She had long, coral-pink hair tied back in twin ponytails. When I pushed it out of the way with a fingertip, the face that appeared was young, breathing peacefully, and solidly in dreamland.

"…What do I do now?"

Frankly, the situation screamed "trouble." First off, I'd only gone into this completely deserted alley because an apple from my bag had rolled this way. Maybe you're thinking, *What a total cliché, that's ridiculous…*, but that's how it goes with me.

"Well, it's not like I can get out of it anyway."

Experience had taught me that once I'd stumbled into trouble, that trouble wouldn't go away until I resolved it. That meant the best plan was to deal with it as quickly as possible.

Besides, since I'd spent a lot of time overseas (partly because I'd had this annoying issue for ages), I could get around passably well in the languages of several countries, so even at times like this, I was able to speak to strangers without hesitating.

"Hey. You alive?" I poked at the girl's cheek with a fingertip.

It was soft, soft and supple and springy as mochi.

"…Nn…uhn…"

The girl squirmed, and the sheets of newspaper covering her rustled. I reached in from the side and poked her cheek again. *Rustle. Poke. Rustle. Poke.* After a few rounds of that…

"Nn, who is it…?"

Finally, the girl sat up, moving sluggishly and rubbing her eyes. Then she turned her head about ninety degrees to the side, and our eyes met.

Hers were large and strong-willed, with long eyelashes. She seemed to be about twelve or thirteen—a cute little girl now, but I had the feeling she was going to be really beautiful someday.

I was examining her closely, when—

"—Oh."

Suddenly, as if she'd realized something, the girl squeezed her eyes shut.

"I'm going to get assaulted."

For some reason, I had an extremely bad feeling about this, but I asked her anyway.

"By who?"

"You!"

The girl glared at me sharply. She'd teared up a little.

"Make no mistake—no matter what you do to my body, you'll never control my heart!"

And now I was the target of a baseless suspicion… Not fair.

"You even dragged me into a back alley… You're the worst! You beast!"

You were sleeping here all on your own. Argh, my head hurts.

"Sorry, but I don't have a thing for little kids."

"—! Wh-who are you calling a little kid?!"

"You."

The girl tried to grab me by the shirtfront, but she was way too short for it to work as a threat.

"Ghk, take that! And that!"

She bounced up and down, attempting to shove her index fingers at my face. Was she trying to blind me or something? This was one dangerous little girl.

"I'm not *little*! I'm a *regular* girl!"

"Yeah, okay, okay. I get it, just calm down."

I caught the girl's wrists, lifting her off the ground so that her feet dangled in midair.

"When you meet someone new, you're supposed to start with introductions. My name is Kimihiko Kimizuka. And you are…?"

"I'm..."

The girl frowned for a moment.

"...Alicia?"

"Why'd you say it like a question? Did you come from Wonderland or something?"

"I'm hungry."

"This is barely a conversation."

I handed her one of the apples I'd just bought. *Would this make her Snow White?* As Alicia nibbled on the crisp red fruit, she finally began looking around curiously.

"So, where are we?"

"What do you mean? Didn't you pick this place to sleep?"

"......"

Once again, I got a bad feeling—and a few seconds later, that feeling proved to be right on the money.

"...I dunno."

Figures. Apparently, she wasn't just lost or a street kid.

"Amnesia," I said.

For the first time, the girl's gaze wandered, uneasily.

I asked about her parents' names. Where she was from. Her birthday. Her friends. What she'd had for dinner last night. I asked plenty of other questions, too, but the girl shook her head at everything.

"All I remember is that I'm seventeen this year."

"You're definitely wrong about that, so forget it ASAP."

"...Where are you looking?"

"It's all right. When the time comes, they'll grow."

But this was no time for bantering. I needed to hurry up and get to work on this problem.

"Once you're done eating, we're going to the police."

Alicia reached for a third apple (guess she was really hungry), and just then—

"Hey, c'mon, really? Just my luck."

Although the sky had been clear just a minute ago, rain suddenly began pelting down. Great. Well, just gotta roll with it.

"Let's run."

"Huh?"

Pulling Alicia by the hand, I made for the apartment where Siesta was waiting.

"Listen, keep it down, all right?"

As I turned the doorknob, I gave Alicia a warning.

"Is there somebody here besides you, Wolf?"

"Don't treat people like animals. I'm Kimizuka, Kimihiko Kimizuka."

I had no idea what Siesta would say if she found out I'd picked up an unidentified little girl.

For now, I'd let her shower, and I'd dry her wet clothes while she was in there. I could take her to the police after that. I tiptoed down the hall, showing Alicia to the bathroom.

"Man, did we get soaked."

"We certainly did. This is awful."

In the changing room, I took off my shirt, and just as I was about to pull Alicia's dress off over her head—

"??!! Why are you acting like you're coming in with me?!"

"Are you dumb?! I told you not to yell."

"Things were happening so naturally, I almost fell for it!"

"I told you, I don't mess around with little kids like you."

"Wha—…?!" Alicia's face turned as red as a boiled octopus.

"Assistant, are you back?"

Just then, I heard Siesta's voice from the living room. *Yeesh, I guess I should back down here.*

"Okay, Alicia. Once you get out, change into some of the spare clothes over there."

With that, I headed for the living room by myself, drying my head off with a towel as I went.

"Welcome back. It's really coming down, isn't it?" she said.

"Yeah, it just hit out of nowhere… What are you doing?"

In the kitchen, which opened onto the living room, Siesta was sitting in a wheelchair and mixing some sort of dough in a bowl. She was good at housework, but I'd almost never seen her cook before. That apron was a novel look on her.

"I thought I'd make an apple pie. You'd said you were going to the trouble of buying some apples, so…"

Siesta's hands moved cheerfully.

"......Oh."

I'd completely forgotten. I'd let Alicia eat all the apples.

"Umm, look. Siesta, uh…"

"Heh-heh! I mean, you know, you seem to have taken quite a liking to me, after all. I suppose this is my way of taking responsibility for being the object of someone's affections; I thought I could do this much for you, at least."

Oh geez. It's even harder to bring up now. Why does she seem genuinely happy, of all things? Ordinarily she gives me about as much thought as the average flea…

"But you came back at just the right time. Well? Where are the apples?"

"Uh, the thing is…"

"Kimizukaaaa."

That was when the voice of a third party broke in. I could think of only one other person who was in this apartment.

"Are there any small towels?" Alicia, wrapped in a bath towel, peeked in around the door frame.

I see. I see, I see.

I stole a glance at Siesta, and our eyes met. There was a silence that seemed to stretch on forever. Then, finally, she hit me with the four-letter word I'd been anticipating.

"—Pedo."

Looks like this might be my last day as her assistant.

◆ A new case opens with a scene straight from hell

"I understand the situation."

Siesta spoke from her perch on the bed, where she was sipping tea. However, even as she said it, she was eyeing me contemptuously.

"Darjeeling, huh? That smells nice."

"Mm-hmm. It goes very well with apple pie."

I'd been trying to put her in a good mood, and instead I'd ended up digging my own grave. This was just not my day.

"It's safe to assume you'll never see me in an apron again."

"No way—you've got to be kidding me. That's all I've been looking forward to my whole life. This is tragic."

"...And now I'm quite angry. Apparently, even an individual of such noble character as myself has room to grow as a person."

"One of an assistant's jobs is fostering the emotional growth of his employer... Okay, okay, I overstepped, just please put that musket away! I'm sorry!"

I knelt by the bed, swearing I'd make it up to her someday and bowing my head to the muzzle of the gun she'd shoved at me.

"I didn't realize you had a girlfriend, Kimizuka," commented Alicia, the girl who'd caused all this trouble. Thanks for that.

She was sitting at the table, munching on apple pie (without the apples). You think I'd date a girl who would turn a gun on me?

"Actually, there was no need to be so roundabout. You should have just brought her to me in the first place." Finally putting her weapon away, Siesta gestured for me to raise my head. "She's a lost girl with amnesia. Doesn't that sound like a job for a detective?"

...*True. Now that she mentions it, she's right.*

"You said you were Alicia?" Siesta called from the bed to the girl at the table. "You really don't know your actual name or anything?"

"...Uh-uh. Just that I'm seventeen this year."

"Seven, okay."

"Seven*teen*!"

Alicia smacked the table, standing up. She must have been at that age where she wanted to be seen as an adult.

"Well, in reality, she's probably about twelve or thirteen. You can tell from her calves."

"Assistant, this isn't the time to show off your peculiar habits. Normal people can't tell how old a person is by the growth of their calves."

"—! So back there in the alley, you were looking at my calves, not my chest?!"

"No, that time, it was your chest. I saw it and thought, 'Nah, there's no way she's seventeen.'"

"O-oh, phew, you had me worried. My chest, huh? Thank goodness... —Wait, no, that's not okay!"

"Assistant, if you must sexually harass someone, limit yourself to Charlie, all right?"

In a distant foreign country, I heard a beautiful blond girl deliver a very colorful retort.

...But now wasn't the time for that.

"Alicia, we'll take on the task of identifying you." Resuming the main topic, Siesta turned to Alicia. "But not for free."

"Hey, Siesta, you're going to take money from a kid?"

"What does her age have to do with it? Children are people, too," Siesta retorted. "Besides, I doubt there's anything less trustworthy than good deeds done for free."

...She had a point. Human relationships really were ninety-nine percent trust and one percent self-interest. That was how Siesta and I had gotten by during our journey, too.

"Then what do you want me to do?"

Alicia probably couldn't pay us with money. She didn't even have food, clothing, or shelter. How could she compensate an ace detective?

"I want you to be my proxy, Alicia. If you do, I promise to provide you with food, clothes, and a place to stay."

"So I'm gonna work as a detective...?" Alicia cocked her head somewhat melodramatically.

"...Siesta, isn't that going to be too much for her? I don't see how this would work."

"Yes, but..."

Siesta pointed to her own injured legs. *Ah, right. The ace detective's on leave right now, huh?*

"In that case, wouldn't it be better if I was the detective, and Alicia was my assistant?"

"No, but, well... Oh, you know what I mean. You just *look* like an assistant."

"That wasn't fair."

"You want me to become a detective out of nowhere?" said Alicia. "I'm not sure I even can..."

"If you're a detective, you'll have my assistant at your beck and call."

"Woohoo! I'll do it! Sign me up!"

"This transaction officially sucks."

Correction: With Siesta and me, the relationship is one percent trust and ninety-nine percent self-interest.

"So what should I do, specifically?" Alicia asked Siesta.

And with perfect timing—

"Jack the Ripper has revived again."

The voice of a third party broke in, and a chill ran through me. I hastily turned around, and—

"Ms. Fuubi? What're you…? Didn't you go back to Japan already?"

Ms. Fuubi, our police officer acquaintance, was sitting on the sofa with a cigarette.

"Oh, well, I remembered I had to see a man about a dog. Anyway, when did you two make a kid?" Ms. Fuubi glanced between me and Siesta, then at Alicia.

"Are you blind?"

"You're blind."

Siesta and I retorted in unison. How could anybody possibly think Siesta and I were in that kind of relationship? *Geez… And she hasn't even quit smoking.*

"So, what did you need? You said something about Jack the Ripper coming back to life."

"Right. A new heart-hunt victim turned up yesterday. The M.O.'s similar to the earlier incidents."

"That's ridiculous…"

I mean, it wasn't even possible. After all, Hel had killed Cerberus—the real Jack the Ripper.

"Hel." On the bed, Siesta narrowed her eyes.

"Oh, that's what's going on…"

Hel had taken up the heart-hunt in Cerberus's place. She was planning to revive that biological weapon again.

"It looks like you've got an idea about what this is. Well, that's perfect. I've actually got some information that might be useful in cornering our perp," said Ms. Fuubi. "This involves the young lady over there, too."

Maybe she'd heard us talking about letting Alicia handle the job. And then she'd brought us an incident that might end up being part of that job.

"This is still just a rumor, but it sounds like there's something here in London that may help us bring down SPES."

Oh-ho. Well, isn't that convenient...? My eyes met Siesta's. Then, when we wordlessly signaled for Ms. Fuubi to go on, she told us what it was called.

"From what I'm told, people call it 'the sapphire eye.'"

◆ The daily routine of proxy detective Alicia

The next day.

"All right, let's go!"

A young girl pointed briskly down a broad downtown avenue, then set off.

Meanwhile, I followed my new employer, my shoulders hunched from awkwardness.

"Come on, step lively!"

"You're stepping too lively."

"Huh?"

Don't 'Huh?' me. And don't tilt your head and look adorably confused.

"That outfit."

Alicia was dressed in a costume that screamed "ace detective": an austere trench coat and deerstalker hat. In addition, she had a traditional Japanese *kiseru* pipe between her lips...well, really a candy with a long, thin stick that she was using as a substitute.

"I know they say to dress for the job you want, but this is ridiculous."

"But these are hand-me-downs from Siesta."

Et tu, Siesta? Didn't know the ace detective had a past.

"You're really going for this proxy detective thing, huh?"

"Of course!" Alicia planted her hands on her hips triumphantly.

After we'd talked things over yesterday, Alicia had ultimately agreed to take over as detective for the injured Siesta in exchange for clothing, room, and board.

For the moment, we were looking for the "sapphire eye" Ms. Fuubi had told us about. We didn't know any of the details, but the two of us had decided to start by putting in some legwork and conducting a field investigation.

"Let's move out!" Alicia declared, then immediately vanished.

"Huh? ...Hey, wait!"

The next thing I knew, Alicia was sprinting over the pavement for all she was worth. I hastily took off after her and ended up running more than a hundred meters before I finally caught up with her.

"...Hff...hff, why were you sprinting...?"

Alicia didn't care about my problems. "Running is fun!"

She was as hyper as a kid on her first trip to the beach. Her smile was as dazzling as the summer sun, and that was great and all...but can't she spare a thought for the guy who has to keep up with her?

"Listen, you don't even remember who you are. You're basically from Wonderland. Being curious is fine, but listen to what I tell you, too." I couldn't even pretend to smile as I dropped a hand lightly onto Alicia's head. "Besides, remember what that red-headed police officer said? This area isn't very safe right now. No wandering around by yourself."

According to Siesta's deduction, Hel was probably still here in London, covertly attacking its residents in Cerberus's place. There was no telling when she'd target Siesta and me again. If Alicia was going around with us, she needed to be careful.

"All right, I get it! Don't treat me like a kid."

That is exactly what a stereotypical kid would say. "Okay. Good girl. Let's go, then."

"Uh-huh... Hey, why did you take my hand?! You were so smooth about it that you almost tricked me again!"

"Come on, Alicia, raise your hand while we're in the crosswalk."

"What exactly do you picture when you think 'thirteen-year-old'?! I mean, seventeen! ...Probably." She sounded less and less certain, most likely because of the memory loss.

"Hmm, I'm pretty sure I was about that age, but..."

When we'd finished crossing at the light, Alicia ran up to a show window and examined her reflection in it. She pulled at her marshmallow-soft cheeks, then tilted her head in puzzlement.

"C'mon, let's go. If she finds out we've been dawdling, Siesta's going to take my butt again and...... Uh."

"...What about your butt? 'Again'? What exactly do you two do, normally?"

As we enjoyed our little conversation, the first destination we reached was, for some reason, a jewelry shop.

It hadn't been my idea, of course. According to our new ace detective, this was the only possible place to find sapphires. Elementary, indeed.

The second we entered the shop, Alicia was off. The way she pounced on shiny things reminded me of a cat.

"Kimizuka! I found it!" Alicia shouted to me excitedly. I really wished she wouldn't; people were giggling at us.

"...Oh. Yeah."

The jewel, which shone as blue as the ocean, cost a whole two zeroes more than I'd thought it would.

"Case closed!" Alicia flashed a peace sign pose, then spoke to one of the clerks: "This one! Cash, one payment."

"Whoa, whoa! Are you planning to make me buy that?!"

"You won't?"

"I can't!"

"...Are you poor, Kimizuka?"

Shut up, all right? And don't give me that pitying look.

"Besides, this is just a jewel. What we're looking for is more... Probably something more 'underground,' say."

"Underground... Okay, got it!"

Alicia flew out of the shop, pulling me by the hand.

"You don't get it! I'm positive you don't get it, so stop, please..."

After another round of involuntary sprinting (at least for me), we reached a shop that was literally underground, in the basement of an old mixed-use building that stood in an alley. I sensed something sketchy about the place, but I pushed open the heavy door anyway. Inside, the store's steel shelves held an array of *dried plants* and *colorful incense*. At the back of the store, a male clerk with several facial piercings was smoking a pipe.

"This is the place! There's no mistake!"

"Except for all the ones in your head."

...Seriously, why are you so energetic? Do you understand the situation you're in?

Yesterday, when you learned you'd lost your memory, you were shaken. That I can understand. But now you're in full "ace detective" mode. You've thrown

*yourself into your new identity. I mean, maybe that's better for your mental
health than staying depressed, but still.*

"Hmm, this looks sweet."

"Are you an idiot?! You'll never kick the habit!"

Hastily, I pulled her out and back up to street level. Felt like we'd been
holding hands this whole time…

"Haaah, I'm exhausted."

This wasn't fieldwork; it was babysitting. But Alicia stalked forward
confidently, completely oblivious to the stress I was under.

"You look like you're having fun."

"Yes, I am." She was beaming so bright that sarcasm seem pointless.
"After all, it's been a long time since I got to go outside."

"Is that right?"

…A long time? What does she mean?

"Huh?" Alicia noticed the strangeness of her own remark and paused,
frowning. "Wait, what made me think that?"

"Did you spend a whole lot of time in a room somewhere? Don't tell me
it was a hospital…" Maybe she'd been hospitalized, then slipped out of her
room and went wandering around the city until she collapsed?

If that was true, it would change the situation. *Should we take her to see a
doctor after all?*

"Mm, I don't know… Whenever I try to think, my head starts to…"

She didn't seem to be lying. Maybe it would be better to just keep an eye
on the situation for now.

"You don't have to force yourself to remember," I said.

In some cases, time resolved this sort of thing naturally. Besides, once
her injuries were healed, Siesta would probably do a little investigating
anyway.

"Oh!" Alicia trotted off to another point of interest, apparently headache-
free again.

"What's up?"

It seemed to be a street stall. There was a mat spread on the paving
stones, with handmade accessories displayed on it.

"This."

She was pointing at a ring set with a sapphire…well, a blue stone that
loosely resembled one.

"It looks similar, but it's not quite the same thing."

I couldn't exactly say the word *fake* in front of the shop owner, so I vagued it up instead.

"I see. So it's not it…"

Alicia's shoulders drooped with obvious dejection. This girl didn't just wear her heart on her sleeve; she waved it on a flag.

"Well, you don't usually find these things right off the bat." I consoled her with a cliché remark.

But it was probably true: We wouldn't find the sapphire eye. More accurately, we didn't really need to find it in the first place.

Then why had Siesta assigned Alicia this job, you ask? *To build a relationship based on that one percent of self-interest.* So that Alicia would be able to depend on us without feeling like she was imposing. She'd probably just used the information Ms. Fuubi had brought in order to set up *an equivalent exchange*: Alicia would be provided with food, clothing, and shelter in return for searching for the sapphire eye. Siesta seemed unsympathetic, but she was considerate of others.

"We should probably head back soon… Wait, huh?"

Yet again, Alicia had vanished as soon as I took my eye off her.

"Forget the sapphire. Finding *her* is gonna be a job and a half…"

When I glanced at the shop owner questioningly, they pointed toward my left.

"…Argh, I forgot."

It was just one damn thing after another. Apparently, this busy day wasn't over yet.

◆ Underage alcohol and tobacco use is strictly prohibited by law

"All right, a toast to Siesta's full recovery. Cheers!"

Siesta, Alicia, and I clinked our glasses together in a pub full of lively music.

It had already been two weeks since our battle with Hel and our meeting with Alicia. The casts had been removed from Siesta's legs, and now, she could walk without any trouble. Today, we'd been partying since this afternoon, ostensibly to celebrate her recovery.

"...I don't even remember how many toasts that makes."

I was pretty sure this was the fourth place we'd been to since noon. My stomach was already filled to capacity, but the ace detectives still hadn't had enough to eat and were scrutinizing the menu seriously. I'd just assumed we were on our last drink, but maybe not.

"There's something I think you'd like, though, Kimi."

"Oh yeah? Okay, just get me that, then."

Without even glancing at the menu, I left my order to Siesta, who was sitting across from me.

"Hmm, it's already nine, though... Don't get anything spicy, Siesta."

"Oh, you're right. Don't want to give myself a stomachache so that I can't sleep again."

"Spicy stuff always gives you the runs about three hours after."

"Huh, I never noticed until you mentioned it to me. That's so weird."

"Look, just take some antacids. You're not done eating yet, right?"

"All right. I'll do that."

Nodding in agreement, Siesta swallowed the medicine. In the meantime, I raised a hand, calling a waiter.

"Um, you're synched so well, it's kinda scary." For reasons unknown, Alicia was glowering at me across the table. "What's this telepathy thing you've got going? You let Siesta decide everything for you, and when you're the one who tells her something, she listens..."

I see. To a bystander, that exchange had looked peculiar. But I mean, we'd spent a full three years together. We naturally let the other person set the criteria for whether or not we were going to do something. In other words—

"We each trust the other more than we trust ourselves," I murmured absently.

"...So basically, you're one of those sappy coup—"

"Excuse me, I'd like to place an additional order."

Siesta clapped a hand sharply over Alicia's mouth. Alicia kept on mumbling unintelligibly (and in pain) while Siesta coolly told the waiter what she wanted. That's an ace detective for you: Even with kids, she shows no mercy.

Before long, Siesta finished her order and released Alicia.

"Haah." Alicia panted. "That hurt... I thought I was going to die..."

"It's your own fault for making fun of adults."

"For an adult, you're really bad at adulting! ...Haah, I'm thirsty." Alicia drained the glass that was closest to her and opened the drink menu. Guess she was still thirsty. "Hey, Kimizuka? What's this 'Cinderella' thing?"

"Hmm? Oh, it's a cocktail. It's non-alcoholic, so even kids can have it."

"Except I'm seventeen, not a kid."

"Seventeen-year-olds aren't allowed to drink, either."

"Then I'll have the Cinderella! Excuse me!" Alicia called, waving a waiter over again... Sheesh, her emotions were a roller coaster.

For the past two weeks, I'd gone all over London with proxy detective Alicia, taking a variety of cases. None of the incidents had been anything major, but I'd been partnered with Alicia, who did whatever her emotions dictated. The work had been littered with hardships that were nothing like what I ran into when Siesta was my partner. Looking back over these two weeks, it felt as if we'd spent every day causing a hundred issues in order to solve one problem.

"What's the matter?" Before long, Alicia noticed me watching her and tilted her head.

"Nothing. I was just thinking how glad I am we found you a place to go home to for a bit."

The trials and tribulations of these two weeks had not been completely fruitless—we'd decided that Alicia would leave the apartment where Siesta and I lived and stay at a certain church. The church ran a charity that took in orphans, and since Alicia had no relatives, they'd agreed to accept her.

"Well, it's only a temporary measure. Until we know about Alicia's memories and identity, we haven't fundamentally resolved the issue," said Siesta, her knife and fork pausing over her roast.

Apparently the fact that she hadn't actually completed the job yet bothered her, but she'd been too injured to do much. She'd negotiated with the church behind the scenes; that was more than enough.

"I went to the church yesterday, and it was a lot of fun," Alicia said to Siesta, maybe sensing her discomfort. "I got to play with some other kids who didn't have families there. It kinda felt like school." Alicia grinned and flashed a peace sign at us.

Apparently even Siesta couldn't argue with a face like that; her lips softened. "School, huh? ...I haven't been there in quite a while, either."

My last memory of it was that cultural festival, back in the second year of junior high. Come to think of it, Siesta had yanked me around quite a lot back then, too.

"And why are you looking at me?" Siesta asked, narrowing her eyes unhappily. "The crepes and the takoyaki were delicious, weren't they?"

"All I remember is my stomachache."

"Yes, you did hole up in the bathroom, didn't you."

"Come to think of it, you peeped on me..."

"And you got scared in the haunted house."

Some memories are better left buried, okay? Also, what was it... If I remembered right, we'd ended up cosplaying a wedding ceremony... No, that wasn't something I wanted to actively remember, either. My dark past.

"Well, the ribbon did look good on you, I guess." I recalled that red-ribbon headband and how it had looked on Siesta.

"You certainly did seem captivated."

"I wasn't captivated. I was just...a little captivated, that's all."

"Assistant. English," Siesta retorted and dabbed at her lips briskly with a napkin.

Hmm? Had I said something weird?

"A ribbon. Lucky..." Alicia was swinging her legs lazily. Apparently, the girl from Wonderland was at an age where she wanted to dress up.

"I'll give you one later," said Siesta.

"Really?! Yay!"

Alicia kicked her legs harder, as if she couldn't contain her excitement, and then—

"I want to wear that, too, and—!" Her voice suddenly lowered. "...And go to a real school," she said with a lonely smile.

Alicia claimed she'd lost her old memories, but that comment sounded as if she was subconsciously aware that she'd never been to school at all.

I couldn't find anything tactful to say to her. Meanwhile, Siesta's blue eyes were narrowed in thought.

"Kidding." However, that shadow only lasted a moment before Alicia energetically drained the contents of her glass. "I don't really care. I've got something else to do now."

"You mean the detective job?"

"Yeah. I don't have time to go to school." Alicia nodded.

"And yet I hear you haven't found the sapphire eye yet," Siesta interjected with a slightly belligerent smile.

She was right. Over the past two weeks, Alicia and I had pulled off really simple requests, such as finding lost pets, but we still hadn't made any headway with the hunt for the sapphire eye.

But Siesta probably wasn't seriously trying to get Alicia to do anything about that. She'd only said that to lighten the mood before it could get too dark—or so I'd thought, but...

"—I—I know that. I just have to find it, right?" Alicia stood up, puffing out her cheeks indignantly. *What are you, an instant water heater?*

"Hey, whoa, you're heading out now?"

"You don't have to come, Kimizuka."

"It's dark outside. There'll be monsters and stuff."

"...Maybe I'll go home first, then head out early tomorrow morning."

Okay, that about-face was so quick that it was actually pretty cute.

"...Ahem. Anyway, I am most definitely going to find it by tomorrow!" Alicia pointed sharply at Siesta and me, then turned on her heel and left.

"She didn't drink her cocktail."

Well, there were bound to be all sorts of other opportunities. I finished what was left in my glass with some relief.

"She's a pretty tricky girl to deal with, isn't she?" Siesta held a fresh glass out to me; no telling when she'd ordered it. "These past two weeks must have been rough."

"You said it... Even if you maybe shouldn't be the one saying it."

Siesta and Alicia's personalities and stances were complete opposites, but they were definitely both tiring people to be with.

"What are we going to do about her from now on, though?" Now that Alicia wasn't here, I chose that moment to ask. I kept the wording vague, but I knew Siesta would understand.

"Once I start a job, I never back out."

"...I see."

If Siesta's injuries were healed, that meant we were ready to fight Hel again. In other words, parting ways with Alicia soon was inevitable.

However, Siesta had shaken her head. She'd chosen to help a lone girl in distress over defeating a great evil.

"I couldn't possibly back down before we've managed to help her learn her age, or where she came from, or even what her real name is. No matter what, I won't let a client's request go unfulfilled." Siesta smiled.

And so our hectic yet peaceful routine was going to last a little longer.

"Then we'll be staying in London for a while?"

"Yes, probably. Just the two of us in the apartment again." Siesta lifted her glass to her lips and swallowed audibly, her white throat working. The motion was rather bewitching.

"What?"

"...Nothing. I was just thinking this was kinda peaceful."

For close to three years, Siesta and I had lived through some turbulent times, pursuing SPES or being pursued by them. We'd walked through deserts without water, we'd slept out in the open during a hurricane, and I didn't have enough fingers to count all the times we'd had to do our business in a field. It had been a dizzying three years, sometimes fighting with pseudohumans, sometimes fighting the limits of human dignity. For me, those days were so—

"You're getting sentimental."

Siesta poked my cheek with a fingertip. She was wearing that expression that said she'd found prey that was worth teasing... I swear, she was as much of a mind-reader as ever. *I really hate that side of you, you know.*

"That's not it." I chugged the contents of the glass Siesta had set in front of me, and then—

"Bfft! —This is alcohol!"

Damn, it's bitter... That was the first liquor I'd ever had.

"Hey, we're minors!"

"You think minors carry one of those around?" Siesta shot a glance at my waist.

Well, if she was going to bring that up, I mean...

"This is my party, remember? You're going to keep me company until I'm done," said Siesta, swirling her glass as if she'd been drinking red wine all her life.

"That's not something a minor should be saying."

"What about you, Kimi? What are you having?"

"No, I'm already..."

"You're going to make it up to me, aren't you?" Siesta's lips moved slightly.

Make what up to her? Is she talking about the apple pie incident?

"You'll do what I say, won't you?" Siesta tilted her head, delicately.

Her cheeks were flushed, and her eyes were faintly moist—maybe it was the alcohol. Somehow, she looked younger than usual.

"...Just one more drink."

After all, I couldn't say no to that, could I?

◆ Later on, I'll remember this day

"And so theeen, I was still little, so I got really nervous when I swallowed the watermelon seed. I thought it might sprout in my stomach, and *then* what would I do?"

After we'd returned from the pub, Siesta's face was so red that her original skin tone was completely lost. She was sitting on the bed with her legs splayed out in an M-shape, bouncing up and down, even though she'd been injured just the other day. She was wearing a bathrobe, just like I was, and every time she bounced, certain *other* parts bounced dramatically, too.

...Or maybe they only seemed to because my head wasn't really working, either.

I didn't know. I couldn't seem to figure it out. After all, I was drunk, too.

I was pretty sure that, at that restaurant with its view of the city lights, we'd promised "Just one more drink," then promised again... About ten times, I think. For the last one, we might have pinky-sworn, linked our arms, and drained our glasses. *Urgh, I can't remember...*

"Assistant? Are you listening to me?"

"Yeah, I'm listening. You were talking about whether a watermelon was a vegetable or a fruit, right?"

"Mm-hmm. I asked for a melon, but then they brought me a *lemon*. I had no idea what was going on."

Desperately forcing my sluggish brain to function, I sat in a chair facing Siesta, nodding along with her story.

Our conversation had been barely functional for a while now, and I kinda suspected she'd been telling me an extremely tedious story, but there was just no way Siesta—flawless, calm, cool, and collected Siesta, the greatest ace detective in history—would dribble on about anything pointless.

Probably just too high-minded for me, I thought, so I kept my eyes locked on hers and listened carefully. Siesta's eyes drooped in a liquid, melting way, and there wasn't a trace of her usual cool image to be seen.

"Say, why have you been so far away all this time?" Siesta pouted sulkily, and I felt as if I was doing something bad somehow. "Come over here."

"...Into bed?"

"Yes. Let's talk over here together, okay?"

I...wasn't sure about that idea.

A young man and woman, getting into bed together... Couldn't that, um, be a problem? In multiple ways?

I tried to harness what little solid thoughts and reason I had left, but—

"Is it not okay?" she asked.

"Nah, it's fine."

If that was the answer my brain had coughed up, then that was the answer I'd give. Obeying the results of my thought experiment, I slipped into the bed Siesta was sitting on.

...Did I actually need to get into *bed?* The thought crossed my mind, and then it promptly vanished.

"Heh-heh. This is the first time we've slept together like this, isn't it?"

Then Siesta got under the covers beside me, and there we were. In the same bed, under the same blankets.

"You're right here, Kimi. So close." Siesta rolled onto her side, gazing at me.

The lights in the room were dim, but I could make out her face clearly.

"If I went two days without seeing you, I really would forget your face."

"So that doesn't change even when you're drunk, huh?"

"Heh-heh. Well, picking on you is fun, Kimi."

"There she is, the young sadist."

"The truth is that you like it when I pick on you, though."

"Don't make up weird motivations for me!"

"Then would you rather I never teased you again, as long as we live?"

"......"

"Should I just not talk to you?"

"......"

"You really are funny, Kimi."

"...Shove it."

"That crabby face is kinda cute."

"That's not a compliment!"

"Well, I'll forget it in two days, though."

"So now we're back to that?!" I rolled over toward Siesta.

"But..."

What I saw was her profile; she was gazing at the ceiling.

"I'll never forget these three years I spent with you."

I don't think I'll ever forget the bravery on her face as long as I live.

"Heh-heh. Whoops, I got a little serious, there."

However, Siesta promptly reverted to her blind drunk expression and rolled over toward me.

"If they took seriousness away from you, what would you have left?" I asked.

I'd missed my chance to revert to my former position, and Siesta and I ended up lying there face-to-face.

"That's so mean. Just what do you think I am anyway?"

Logic incarnate? The cerebral ace detective or something? Was that what I should say?

"Why don't we..."

Smoothly, Siesta closed the distance between us.

Just a few more centimeters and our noses—and possibly our lips—would touch. Our bodies were already almost pressed together, and from the swell of Siesta's ample bosom, I could hear the sound of her leaping heart.

"...do something silly for a change?"

My whole body grew hot.
Come to think of it, we'd discussed her three great drives at one point.
"Siesta, I'm..." The next thing I knew, I was leaning over Siesta.
"...Assistant." Siesta shut her eyes, tightly.
Making up my mind, I brought my face, my lips, closer to her, closer—

◆ Most late-night moments of weakness make you want to die in the morning

"Phew, someone kill me, please."
When I woke up the next morning, after a minute or so of attempting to think, that was the first comment that came to mind.
First things first—my head hurt like a bitch; last night's alcohol was definitely still in my system. And that headache was figurative and literal, thanks to the ace detective fast asleep next to me, breathing peacefully.
I'd heard that when you drank enough liquor to fill a bathtub, you forgot everything by the next morning...but unfortunately, my cerebral cortex remembered yesterday's sorry display with devastating clarity.
"Uu, ghk, kill me noooow..."
My first-ever drinking binge had combined with the late-night mood to create a mortifying exchange. What the hell had I been thinking yesterday? What had made me get into bed with Siesta? And after that...
"Bluuurgh."
Various emotions and the contents of my stomach forced their way up in a wave of nausea. Clapping a hand over my mouth, I started to get out of bed, and just then—
"......"

Siesta's eyes opened, and we made eye contact. We gazed at each other, blinking, for a moment that seemed to stretch on forever.

"...Good morning."

"......"

I greeted her tentatively, but there was no response.

Instead, Siesta ducked under the covers, checking on something. Then she poked her head out again. Her expression was unreadable. That part was fairly normal...but for some reason, I could nearly sense something like menace in it.

"Good morning," Siesta answered after an eternity. Firmly securing her bathrobe around her, she took a small silver attaché case out of the suitcase she always used.

I couldn't see exactly what she was doing, since she was facing away, but I assumed she was taking something out of the case. Just as I thought that, Siesta turned back to me.

"Assistant, I want you to hold out your arm."

"Maybe after you put the huge needle away!"

Siesta was holding a syringe in her right hand; there was liquid leaking out of its tip. "It's fine. It'll only hurt for a second."

"Hell no! When I said I wanted to die, I wasn't being serious!"

"It won't kill you. This injection temporarily erases human memories, that's all."

"You're kidding, right?! Is that another one of your special Seven Tools?!"

"No, it's not. Come on, don't you remember? At the cultural festival, where we caught the Miss Hanakos. This has just a little of the same ingredient that was in that *drug* mixed into it."

Th-this couldn't be worse... That stuff's guaranteed to work...

"It's fine. I've run some experiments and made an improved version that won't damage your health."

"Wait just a minute, did you run those on me?! I thought I'd been more forgetful than usual lately; was that why?!"

If it was, this was no joke. Still in my bathrobe, I tried to bolt out of the apartment, but—

"I won't let you get away."

"Ghk, hah." Siesta leaped onto my back, straddling me and pinning me to the floor.

"Now put out your arm. You're going to forget everything about yesterday… About *me* yesterday."

I was no match for a ticked-off Siesta, and the syringe bore down on my right arm—

Ding-dong. At the very last second, the doorbell rang, announcing a visitor.

"…Somebody's here."

"……"

"You're sure you don't need to get that?"

"Tch!"

"Don't *tsk* at me; just…don't." *It's totally out of character for you.*

Getting off me reluctantly, Siesta headed for the door. "Yes?"

When she opened it, standing on the other side was…

"It was really noisy in here. What were you doing?"

…Alicia, the proxy detective.

"Well, not like I care." She put her hands on her hips and declared, "Mission accomplished."

Alicia surveyed us triumphantly. She was holding a small bag.

Mission accomplished? She couldn't actually have found the sapphire eye after that, could she?

Had Alicia—*our* Alicia—managed to find what Siesta had nearly given up on?

"Here."

Alicia held the bag out to me. Inside was—

"An eye patch?"

It was a perfectly ordinary black eye patch, something that made no sense in the context of the conversation.

"The eye that's actually important is that one, isn't it?" Alicia boldly declared, pointing at my left eye. "Unless you wear an eye patch like you're supposed to, *it won't heal up.*"

Standing on tiptoe, Alicia tied the eye patch on.

"…So you noticed, huh?"

"Well, we were together for two whole weeks."

I hadn't intentionally been hiding it from Alicia, but my left eye had been wounded in that fight with Hel. As far as day-to-day life was concerned, it wasn't much of a problem, but my visual impairment had caused me to lose track of Alicia in town several times.

"That phantom eye may not even exist—instead of relying on it, you should take good care of the one that's already here."

Apparently, I'd misread Alicia a bit as a person. The girl who openly expressed all her emotions was probably just the surface. Her true nature was bound to be—

"That's my answer." Alicia glanced at Siesta. "Is it *the right one*?"

Was that what it had been? Had this been the problem Siesta had set for Alicia all along? Had she wanted to see what sort of answer the girl would come up with, when given the impossible task of finding something that didn't exist? After a short silence, Princess Kaguya of the Bamboo gave her long-awaited answer.

"J-just as I'd planned."

Siesta's gaze was wandering so dramatically it beggared belief.

"No, seriously, how bad at lying are you?"

Even if it was only for a moment, the proxy had outmatched the ace.

◆ The turning point for everything

"I'm not terribly good at being clever in the moment."

Siesta was walking beside me, her expression unusually bitter.

After the episode that morning, Siesta had accompanied me to the supermarket to do some shopping now that her legs were fully healed.

"I haven't seen you like that in a long time," I commented.

The ace detective seemed to be a perfect superhuman, but she had a surprising number of weak points.

"...Shut up."

It was unusual for her to be this cranky, too. It wasn't bad to flip the power dynamic once in a while, was it?

"Do you like your present from a girl that much?" Siesta shot a cold glance at the eye patch over my left eye.

But before I could make some kind of objection—

"…No, sorry. That's not what I meant." Siesta's shoulders hunched just a little, and there was less confidence in her voice than usual. "I'm just embarrassed that I wasn't as attentive about your eye."

"Is that right?"

For a moment, I wasn't sure what to say.

"Well, you know. You're human, too, I guess." I chose something totally obvious. "I'm glad you're human enough to get yanked around by petty emotions like that."

"…Really."

She smiled faintly, then nodded quietly two or three times.

After that, we walked on for a while, and then Siesta abruptly stopped. She was studying the sign for an underground live music venue. There was a poster for a performer pasted to the wall nearby—and although it didn't give their name, it advertised an upcoming guest from Japan.

"Siesta?"

"…It's nothing." Siesta shook her head and started walking again. "Not yet."

"…?"

Just as I was about to ask her what she meant, my cell phone vibrated in my pocket. According to the screen, it was an international call. Wondering what was up, I hit the TALK button and heard a very familiar voice.

"Hey, you damn brat. It looks like you managed to survive somehow."

She talked like a middle-aged man, which was probably why guys tended to avoid such an attractive woman. Telling her so was guaranteed to get me drawn and quartered, though.

"That's what you should have said when we ran into each other earlier, Ms. Fuubi."

Plus, Siesta and I both sustained major injuries because of that Jack the Ripper case you brought us. Earlier, when you randomly appeared in our apartment, you didn't mention that at all.

As I thought back, it struck me as incredibly unfair, and I was planning to continue with a complaint or three, when—

"Huh? When did we run into each other?"

The voice from the phone wasn't teasing. She sounded genuinely bewildered.

"Come on, what are you talking about? It was two weeks ago. You dropped in unannounced and told us something about a sapphire eye, remember?"

"*Huh? I only visited you once, to discuss the Jack the Ripper incident with you. You confuse me with somebody?*"

I broke out in goose bumps all over.

"*I just heard that you two had a hell of a fight after that; this is the first time I've called.*"

Whoa, wait, you're kidding me. What was that, then? Two weeks ago, when we'd met Ms. Fuubi, or the individual who looked like her, for the second time— No, that's right. Come to think of it, there was something weird. When she'd shown up then, she'd had her Zippo lighter, even though she'd given it to me earlier.

"*Hello? Kimizuka? Hellooooo?*"

The voice on the other end of the phone seemed to be getting farther and farther away.

My unpleasant hunch changed to certainty crawling all through me.

"Assistant."

Siesta must have figured out what this conversation was about already. She nodded quietly, her expression grim.

The Ms. Fuubi we'd met in London that second time had been a fake.

There was only one being who could pull off that trick: Cerberus, the shape-shifter.

◆ Ace detective vs. ace detective

It was the day after that phone call with *the real* Ms. Fuubi.

"But Hel definitely killed Cerberus in front of us. Didn't she?" I said.

In a room of our detective office-and-residence…

As Siesta and I poked at our curry, I was trying to get the situation straight in my mind.

"The carrots are as hard as rocks," she complained.

"Yeah, it was a mistake to make me cook, huh?"

"Why do you sound almost proud?"

"The thing is, I couldn't find the usual kitchen knife anywhere."

"…So that's why the vegetables are in chunks. You broke them up with your hands."

Okay, this isn't the time to be arguing about the curry.

"Anyway, you're right. Cerberus died. I doubt there's any mistake about that."

"Then what was that fake Ms. Fuubi? If that was a transformation ability, then Cerberus really can't be…"

"Which view are you backing, Kimi?"

…Well, no matter which theory we went with, we'd have a contradiction on our hands. Cerberus had seemed to die right in front of us—but then there was no way to explain the fake Ms. Fuubi who'd shown up afterward.

"That means they're either both true or both false."

"What is that, a Zen riddle?"

"Don't joke about this." Siesta shoved a spoon with a chunk of potato on it into my mouth. Okay, yeah: This dish was a fail.

"What if our counterfeit cop was actually Hel?"

"Hel? But she didn't have a transformation ability—"

"Here's the thing about pseudohumans," Siesta interrupted. "They're created with a certain object as their core. If they inherit the core, they can inherit its special abilities as well."

"Was that the black rock thing that Hel pulled out of Cerberus's chest?"

"Exactly. It's conceivable that she stealthily retrieved that and stole Cerberus's abilities."

"Then you're saying Cerberus himself is already dead, and Hel inherited his ability, pretended to be Ms. Fuubi, and made contact with us?"

That would explain why the heart hunt was still going on, even though Cerberus had died.

In that case, why on earth had Hel visited us? It was a bold move, coming to talk to the two of us and Alicia.

On top of that, she'd gone out of her way to talk about the serial murders she was committing and tell us about the existence of the sapphire eye. A taunt…? No—from an ordinary perspective, it was more likely to have been a trap.

"We still don't know what the truth is. But what we need to do hasn't changed. We'll put an end to these murders."

Yeah, she was right. We'd defeat Hel for sure this time, full stop.

"By the way, do the victims of the current incidents have anything in common? Or are they random, like Cerberus's were?"

"It looks as if they're attacking passersby at random," said Siesta. "Number four was killed last night."

"So is she going around stealing hearts to revive the biological weapon?"

"I'm not sure. They might be for *herself*."

"For herself? …Oh, I see."

Right. In that last one-on-one fight with Siesta, Hel had pierced her own heart with her blade.

"That being the case, Hel may be going around searching for a replacement heart."

"Can she pull off a dress-up doll trick like that one?"

"She can," Siesta replied casually. "After all, the enemy is a pseudohuman."

…True. We'd been fighting monsters this whole time.

"Still, I'm impressed you managed to find out that much in just a day."

Yesterday, after I'd ended the phone call with Ms. Fuubi, Siesta had vanished into the city by herself. Finally, around dinnertime today, she'd come back with all this information.

"It wasn't easy; they've muzzled the press. Besides, if I'd been at full capacity during those two weeks, I would have picked up on a few things sooner."

"Don't worry about it; rest while you're injured, at least. If you don't, I…"

I broke off. Siesta stole a glance at me.

"No, never mind." I shoveled the nasty curry into my mouth instead of finishing the thought.

Sometimes I worry you might break. To her, my selfish worry would probably just be a nuisance.

"Tomorrow's gonna be a hell of a day," I said to bridge the gap in the conversation.

"True. But in that case…" Unusually, Siesta hesitated. But she didn't have to say it for me to understand.

"Alicia, you mean?"

We'd found a place that would take Alicia in temporarily, but of course that didn't completely resolve the issue. If we threw ourselves into battle with Hel, we'd end up kicking Alicia's problem farther down the road. Siesta was probably concerned about that.

"If this is about me, I'm fine."

Well, if Alicia said so, then we could probably keep our priorities the way they were, but...

"...! A-Alicia, when did you—!"

The next thing I knew, Alicia was on my left, crunching away on the curry I'd made.

"This is way too loud to be curry," she commented.

That was when I finally remembered the eye patch over my left eye. Unless I thought about it, I forgot that my vision was limited.

"Did you wash your hands?"

"Don't treat me like a child. I washed them until my fingerprints wore off."

"What are you, a wanted criminal?"

"Anyway." Alicia returned the conversation to the original topic. "You don't have to worry about me. You should focus on the issue that's killing people."

With unexpected calm (although maybe that's a rude way to put it), Alicia insisted that we should resolve the incidents that were occurring in this city before we dealt with her problem.

"Alicia, what's your game here?" Siesta seemed vaguely skeptical as she observed Alicia. "You didn't go to the trouble of coming here just to say something that sensible, did you?"

...Somehow, I felt like the temperature in the room had dropped a few degrees.

Not to be outdone, Alicia leaned over the table, facing Siesta squarely. "I want you to let me help with this case, too."

"I thought you'd say that. But no, absolutely not."

"Why not?"

"Because it's dangerous. Four people have died already."

"I solved cases with Kimizuka, too. For two whole weeks."

"You mean finding cats and delivering wallets to police boxes?"

"S-size doesn't matter when it comes to cases!"

"That's a bit of a stretch."

"But it's still an argument!"

Their opinions stayed on parallel rails, never intersecting—but physically, the distance between their faces was closing, until they were so close that their noses nearly touched... Although Siesta hadn't moved a millimeter from her original position.

"Calm down a little." I caught Alicia's small shoulder and returned her to her chair.

"...I'm a detective, too." Alicia's shoulders drooped conspicuously. She'd lost that round.

"Alicia, at best, you were a proxy detective." However, Siesta didn't ease up. She just stated the facts. "Now that I've recovered, you aren't needed."

"...Hey, Siesta. Don't you think that's a little harsh?"

What she was saying was correct, but the correct answer wasn't necessarily always the best solution.

"What? You're taking her side, Kimi?"

"You know I didn't say that."

"Oh, so you really do like little girls... Huh, you're right. The carving knife's gone."

"I told you, I don't. Also, don't go looking for sharp objects in the middle of this conversation."

"Then what? You spent three years with me, and now you'd choose her after only two weeks *playing* detective..."

She cut herself off, apparently realizing she really had said too much this time.

"Siesta, what's wrong?"

She was acting weird today.

...No, it wasn't just today. She might have been like that all the time lately.

It was as if she was feeling anxious and impatient, for some reason. But then she'd abruptly turn open and honest, and start acting like she wanted me to baby her. Come to think of it, she'd been striking out on her own more often lately, attempting to get things done without telling me. Was she hiding something from me?

"It's nothing. Nothing's wrong," Siesta replied indifferently from the kitchen.

She didn't turn to look at me. And of course, she didn't answer any of my questions... But that was the relationship we'd built. She wouldn't die without telling me. The simple fact that she'd made that promise to me back then was more than enough progress.

"Fine, then." Alicia stood smoothly. She gazed at Siesta, and her eyes were determined. "I'll do this my way."

In a certain sense, that was her good-bye to Siesta; in another, it was the true birth of the new detective.

"I swear I'll be the one to solve this case. Once I do, I'll—" Alicia bit her lip.

"Alicia?" I said.

She shook her head. "Nothing." Why wouldn't either detective answer questions from her assistant? "Still, that's how it is. Starting tomorrow, I'll be counting on you, Kimizuka."

The request had come out of nowhere, and I had no idea what I'd be helping with, but my employer had put me through a strict daily training regimen—

"Yeah, sure. Roger that; I'm on it."

And so on reflex, I gave a response that wasn't likely to cause offense.

"Hooray! You heard him: Kimizuka's going to be my assistant from now on, too!"

".........Huh?"

The reaction had come from Siesta, who was turning back to look at me and Alicia.

I mean, a mental "Huh?" had gone through my head, too, but the one who'd actually said it aloud was Siesta.

"No, Assistant is my...my..."

She couldn't get out the rest of that sentence. Her lips just moved a little, uselessly.

Right then...

"Sirens?"

A warning of major trouble passed the window.

That sound meant Hel had stolen the heart of a fifth victim.

◆ People call it Jack the Devil

Up until now, the press had been restricted due to fears that attracting more attention to the crimes might escalate them. However, with the fifth victim in this chain of grotesque murders, the modern-day Jack the Ripper—now known as Jack the Devil—was finally exposed to the public eye.

The reason was that, while the first four victims had been killed late at night, this murder had happened at a fairly early hour, in the presence of multiple witnesses. Most importantly, the fifth victim had been a young female member of Parliament who'd been famous in this district.

A charismatic, beautiful politician had been murdered in a gruesome way—the media was scrambling over itself to cover the sensational incident.

"...And this is the result, huh?"

We'd come to the large house where that fifth victim was said to have lived with her mother, but it was already being mobbed by a throng of camera-wielding reporters. I knew I was here because I'd hoped to find a hint of some sort, too, but this was clearly crossing a line.

"Right in the middle of a tragedy..."

As she watched the media completely fail to consider the feelings of the victim's bereaved family, Alicia clenched her small fists next to me.

The crew members banged on the door and leaned on the doorbell so hard, it was a wonder it didn't break. Finally, the door swung open, as if it hadn't been able to take the beating anymore, and a haggard-looking woman of around sixty emerged. The reporters hastily surrounded her.

"Kimizuka, that's..."

"Yeah, it's probably her mother."

The woman shrank back before the mob of cameras on her doorstep.

"...I'm sorry. There's nothing I can tell you..."

But the reporters kept badgering her until the questions almost sounded accusatory.

"Kimizuka..." Alicia tugged on my sleeve gently.

"Yeah, I know."

Just as I was wondering if there was anything we could do to run that crowd off...

Bang! In the distance, I heard the crack of a gunshot.

After that, things moved fast. Scrambling over themselves again, the media crews dashed off in pursuit of fresher information. Less than a minute later, everyone but us was gone.

"Mercenary bunch, aren't they?"

They were like vermin lunging at scattered bait. Blatantly using the instincts of dumb animals—*our ace detective* was a little different from the rest.

"I'm impressed, Siesta."

"Do you feel like returning to me now?" she asked, coming up next to me. She shot me a cold glance.

I don't remember ever dissolving our partnership in the first place, you know.

"...Thanks," Alicia said quietly, temporarily shelving the weird awkwardness in their relationship.

"It's not as if I did it for anyone in particular."

"Oh, just say what you mean."

That, right there. Siesta always said that kind of thing to me. I never thought I'd see her on the receiving end.

"Oh!"

Alicia gave a brief cry, as if she'd noticed something. However, by the time I turned around, she was over by the front door, supporting the woman who'd been attacked by the media.

"Hurry, you two!" Alicia called to us.

The woman had nearly collapsed from the sudden release of tension. Both Siesta and I let her lean on our shoulders as well, and together, we helped her into the house.

"I'm sorry for the trouble I've caused you," the woman said.

We were in the living room now, and resting a little seemed to have helped her.

"I'll go put on the kettle for—"

"No, please don't bother." Shakily, she tried to rise from the sofa.

"Are you okay?" Sitting next to her, Alicia slipped in to support her and lowered her to the sofa again. Siesta and I were sitting opposite them.

"I'm so sorry. It was very sudden, and I'm still shaken..."

The woman gazed at a framed photo that stood on a nearby shelf. In it, she and her daughter—the MP who'd died in this incident—were standing together and smiling.

"My husband died young in an accident, and for so long, I was never able to give that girl anything more than hardship... And yet she told me that one day, she'd be rich enough for her mum to live comfortably. And she did—she grew to be a splendid young woman, and she even built me this house. She was far too good for me, and I was so proud of—"

A sob escaped her, and Alicia rubbed her back gently.

"I want to ask you about the day of the incident," Siesta interjected, even as the woman cried. "Did you notice anything unusual about your daughter?" Her phrasing was matter-of-fact, and her expression didn't change in the slightest. As if she believed that was what she should be doing, Siesta did her *job*.

"...Siesta, listen..."

I saw how I'd misunderstood. She hadn't gotten rid of the media in order to help this woman. She'd wanted to speak to her without anyone getting in the way.

That was how Siesta did things; I'd known that. The intellectual ace detective didn't let fleeting emotions sway her.

"That day...? No. There was nothing particularly unusual before she left the house..."

Dabbing at her eyes with her handkerchief, the mother seemed to find answering the question painful.

"In that case, when you saw your daughter's body, was anything—"

"Siesta."

I wouldn't let her get any further. Siesta glanced at me, then closed her mouth.

"I wasn't able to give her anything," the woman said softly. "I only took what she gave me, and I couldn't give her anything in return. Who'd have thought it would hurt this much? I never dreamed..."

The tears were streaming down her face now. There was nothing Siesta could say. I'd stopped her, but I couldn't find anything to say, either.

"That's not true."

The voice was so tearful that I thought it belonged to the woman at first, but no—it had come from the person who was sitting beside her.

"No one ever only takes, or only gives. No relationship is that one-sided."

Alicia stood up, tears trickling down her cheeks, and spoke to the woman earnestly.

"If you 'only took' something from your daughter—I'm sure it's because you'd given her so much in the past! Isn't that right?! People's feelings always go both ways. That's how it should be."

She had no proof, and possibly not even a persuasive argument—but Alicia used the steady passion that blazed inside her to fuel her words.

Alicia extended a hand to the person she hoped to save. She was the polar opposite of Siesta; I probably couldn't have pulled it off, either.

"...Thank you."

The woman stood up, then gently pulled Alicia into an embrace.

"Somehow, it feels as though my daughter is telling me those things."

◆ For sure, from now on, forever

"About earlier."

We were on our way back home. After a long period of silence, Siesta spoke with some effort.

"Why did you stop me?"

She was probably asking why I'd interrupted her question. I was supposed to be her assistant, so why had I gotten in the way of her work?

"For starters, these incidents are supposedly the work of a random attacker. Meaning it's pointless to ask whether the victim did anything different beforehand."

"We only know that was true of the first four incidents. There's no guarantee that the fifth was the same. I had to ask that question to rule out the possibility that it was an exception."

"Then why ask about the corpse? Asking if she'd noticed anything when she saw the body—that wasn't..."

"It's the same thing. There might have been something besides the removal of the heart, something noteworthy that only family would notice. You blew our chance to verify that." The frustration in Siesta's eyes was like a knife.

What she was saying was logical, objective, and correct. However, "correct" was all it was. Sometimes just being right wasn't enough to save someone.

...I mean, I wasn't exactly thinking that in so many words. As a matter of fact, Siesta's justice had saved me many times.

However, I'd learned there was someone who thought that wasn't everything. Someone who believed that being correct wasn't always top priority.

That had to be why I'd hesitated. Even if maybe I shouldn't have.

"I'll do whatever it takes to defeat Hel. No matter what I have to do, I'll bring her down. That's what I think. But..." Suddenly, a hint of loneliness entered her voice. "I see you're not the same."

"Siesta, I'm..."

"You were the one thing I believed in, you know." Her long lashes were lowered, but I could see the uncertainty in her blue eyes beneath them.

Her expression looked sad, and vaguely resigned.

I wanted to tell her *No, that's not what I meant...* But I couldn't get the words out.

"I'm going home for today." With that, Siesta trudged on ahead.

"Siesta..."

"I'll see you later."

My hand reached out after her, but touched nothing but empty air. Siesta returned to the apartment by herself.

"............But we're going back to the same place." I sighed, alone in the sunset. Tonight was shaping up to be pretty uncomfortable. "Also, quit hiding and come out, Alicia."

I called to the ace detective who was peeking out from the gap between two buildings. She was still very, very bad at tailing people.

"Agh, you figured it out? Weird..." Alicia was seriously puzzled about it as we walked along, side by side.

"Well, you know. That sort of thing happens a lot." Alicia had probably seen Siesta and me arguing, so I told her not to worry about it. "I mean, when you travel together for three years, it's only natural to wind up fighting once or twice. Actually, it would be weirder not to. You know she and I have completely different personalities and lifestyles. In fact, it's pretty impressive that we've lasted three whole years. She's constantly napping, and then she scolds me for waking up cranky. We fight like this basically every day, and... Well, okay, this might actually be the first time it's been this serious, but, um...oh, what's the saying? 'What doesn't kill you makes you stronger.' Maybe we can take this opportunity to deepen our understanding of each other in multiple ways. Uh, I mean, not that I *want* to improve our mutual understanding, really, it's just, like..."

"Wow, you're seriously worried about this." Alicia was staring at me like I'd grown another head. "You've got anxiety written all over your face. And if you were trying to hide your thoughts, it really didn't work."

"...Let's not talk about this anymore, all right?"

If I had Alicia looking at me like that, it was completely hopeless. I'd wipe the last couple of minutes from my memory.

"Oh, come to think of it..." Instead, I remembered something else and started rummaging in the pocket of my pants.

"Yaugh."

"Geez, it's nothing weird. Here." I handed the object I'd taken out to Alicia.

"Huh? Is this— It's the one from back then...?" Alicia carefully examined the ring in the palm of her hand.

It was the ring with the blue stone that she'd found at that roadside stall that one time, while we were looking for the sapphire eye.

"Well, you know. It's not exactly a thank-you present for this, but anyway." I pointed at the patch over my left eye.

The gift was basically just a toy, so I wasn't expecting much of a reaction, but...

"—I'm happy." Alicia closed her eyes, squeezing the ring tightly in front of her chest.

"...Alicia?"

Her small body seemed to be trembling slightly. "It's the first present anyone's ever given me."

"Alicia, don't tell me— Did your memory...?"

But Alicia shook her head. "I get that feeling, though. I think...before I lost my memory, I must have been a bad kid." Alicia smiled thinly.

She was blaming herself, not her environment; she had looked inside herself for the reason she'd never been given a present.

When I heard that self-deprecating comment, I almost reached a hand out toward her head...but at the last minute, I thought better of it.

I wasn't *qualified* to do that. So I bantered the way I always did, to camouflage it. "You make it sound like you aren't a bad kid now."

"—Huh?! I'm an incredibly good kid! I'm chipper and cute and honest and everybody loves me!"

"You crack me up."

"Well, don't!" Alicia pummeled me with both hands, and I let them hit my chest, not even bothering to block them.

She said she was seventeen. She looked thirteen. Emotionally, she was seven.

I gazed at that odd ace detective with *a certain thought* in mind.

"...Hey."

Abruptly, the zero-damage attack stopped, and then a small, thin voice came from the vicinity of my chest.

"Put the ring on," she coaxed, looking up at me.

"Me?"

"Yes, you."

"On you?"

"Yes, on me."

...I hadn't foreseen that possibility. As I was scratching my head, trying to figure out what I should do, Alicia set the ring in my free hand, then stood in front of me and held out her hand, with its back facing me.

"Why your left hand?"

"If you put it on the wrong finger, I'll get mad."

You've got to be kidding me. Why is this vaguely like a proposal?

"...This is just pretend, all right? Pretend."

But I didn't have a choice. I knelt, taking Alicia's slim left hand.

"Speak your vows."

"Why are you being the pastor, too?"

"Heh-heh!"

Don't give me that cute laugh like this is normal. Geez.

I cleared my throat a couple of times, then said the vows, or whatever.

"Well, uh, so, from here on out, or forever, or something... Looking forward to working with you, et cetera."

What the hell was she making me do? This was like one of those games where if you think about it, you lose.

"That was pretty sloppy."

"Shut up. Don't get greedy."

I slipped the ring onto Alicia's ring finger, and just then—

"I said too much back there."

I heard a very, very familiar voice. When I turned to look, I saw the very familiar girl I'd expected—and she started speaking rapidly, her eyes on the ground.

"Well, of course I still don't think my idea was wrong, and I also don't think it's okay to deviate from it that easily. But it's only natural for you to have your own opinions about justice, same as me...and since we are working together as partners, um, sometimes it's necessary for us to compare and adjust our principles... Long story short, what I mean is that it wasn't good for me to try to force you to conform to my own ideas. It was, um, improper, I think, to act like I was disappointed. That said, there really are some things you should reconsider... Um, I'm not trying to rehash the conversation, it's just..."

The girl, who was continuing to make a sorry display of herself in a way that was reminiscent of someone else I knew, finally looked straight ahead, as if she'd made up her mind. I'm sure I don't have to tell you what she saw.

At last, overcoming a silence that had seemed likely to go on forever, she grinned and spoke.

"I hope you'll be very happy together."

Ah, so looks can kill, I thought.

"Kimizuka, thanks for everything you've done for me."

"Agh, yeah, I'm gonna die, aren't I?"

◆ I don't understand you

"Hey, Siesta. Can you hear me?"

"........."

The time was near midnight, and the room was dark.

Siesta was in bed, and I was lying on the sofa. I knew she wasn't asleep; the sheets kept rustling.

"Can't you hear me?" I said. "What, did I die and just not notice? Is that what this is?"

"........."

...And so on and so forth.

It had been three days since that clash, but Siesta's mood still hadn't improved. For those three days, we'd acted completely independently, and we hadn't talked at all. We'd pursued Hel, aka Jack the Devil—Siesta by herself, and me with Alicia. Apparently she didn't like the fact that I was still being Alicia's assistant, either.

"Are you a kid?" I grumbled, finally starting to get upset.

"It's hardly fair of you to insult me like that when you're in love with a little kid, Kimi."

...Geez, finally. Apparently, I wasn't a ghost after all.

"I think an assistant who's been unjustly ignored for three days deserves a little more pity, though."

"No, I didn't realize you were there. I just assumed you'd moved to a country that would let you marry thirteen-year-old girls."

"Don't give me the silent treatment for three whole days for the sake of a single joke. I thought you'd snapped for real."

"Well, I did snap for real, though."

Well, don't. And don't just break character out of nowhere, either.

"Heh-heh. Now that I think back over it, it's all starting to seem rather funny. Why were you proposing by the side of the road?"

"It's rude to laugh at a proposal. Not that that's what it was."

I'd told her and told her it was just a game.

Once again, I explained the conversation I'd had with Alicia, and the circumstances.

"No one had ever given her a present before."

Alicia had been almost giddy to receive it. And so it had only been a game, and...actually, I wonder what she'd thought it was. For the past three days, the sight of Alicia's smile as she held her left hand up at every opportunity had kept surfacing in my mind, then vanishing again.

"Hey, Siesta. You still don't know anything about Alicia, right?"

True, we had our hands full with Hel right now, but maybe Siesta had found something.

"Mm, I haven't got a clue."

For the ace detective, that was unusual. Maybe it was because she hadn't fully thrown herself into the investigation yet.

"But..." I could hear Siesta sitting up. "You know, Kimi, so that's fine, isn't it?"

"What are you talking about?" I asked from the sofa.

I closed my eyes, lest we somehow make eye contact even in the darkness.

"Mm, I haven't got a clue." Siesta repeated the exact same line she'd said earlier.

Just then, my phone vibrated. I'd left it on the table, and I sprang up to check the screen.

"Sorry, Siesta. I'm headed out for a bit."

"It's late. Where are you going?"

I kicked the door open and said, "My fiancée's in trouble."

◆ I don't care if you make fun of me

"Alicia!"

What I saw when I reached my destination was exactly what I'd been afraid of, the worst-case scenario. In a dark alley, under a blinking streetlight, two figures lay on the ground. The one closer to me was Alicia.

I ran to her. "…! Are you okay?!"

She was lying facedown. When I helped her sit up, supporting her with my arm, I saw she was bleeding heavily from her right shoulder. However, I didn't see any other wounds—

"…—Kimi…zuka."

She was conscious, too. *Okay, she'll live*, I thought, and immediately used my cell to call an ambulance.

"What about…him…?" With a trembling hand, Alicia tried to point at something.

Right, what about the other person on the ground…?

"There's a gash in the left side of his chest."

When I moved toward him, Siesta was already performing first aid on the fallen man. She must have followed me here.

"He's unconscious, but I don't think his life is in danger. He's a police officer."

I saw a gun and a knife on the ground nearby. Yeah, I guess a police officer would be wearing a knife-proof vest. It must have kept that wound from being lethal.

"Hey, Assistant?"

"Alicia's safe, too. It was probably the work of Hel…Jack the Devil, but for now, no one's dead. That's good."

"Assistant."

"It looks like the ambulance is here. I'll ride with Alicia, so… You go home and rest, all right?"

Relieved by the sound of the approaching siren, I picked up Alicia's petite body.

"Assistant. Are you all right with that?" Siesta's voice was vaguely sad, and for a moment, it stopped me in my tracks.

However...

"When we get back, let's have apple pie. All three of us."

That childish wish was the only thing I could say.

"...Kimizuka?"

After that, when she woke up in the hospital bed, Alicia rubbed her eyes and noticed my presence.

"Hey, you're awake. Does anything hurt?"

Alicia shook her head. "Kimizuka, I..."

"It's fine."

Alicia tried to sit up, but I held her back on the bed.

"Who'd have thought you'd run into Jack the Devil, huh? From what the doctor says, though, if you rest for a while, you'll heal up. That's some consolation anyway." I took a chilled apple out of the fridge, set a knife against the peel, and began turning it. "The police should be stopping by soon. You were a victim in this incident, so they're probably going to ask you lots of things...but I'll be here, so don't worry. I'll make sure nothing ugly happens."

"Kimizuka."

"Oh, and it sounds like the police officer who was on the ground with you is going to pull through. For the moment, that fifth victim is still the last one. So you just rest easy for a while, and—"

"Kimizuka!"

Alicia grabbed my right arm. A thrill of tension ran through me, but...

"You're down to the core."

"...Peeling apples is hard."

I put the slices, which were now very small, on a plate.

"Aaaaaah."

"What, you too?!"

Pretty sure I've seen this one before. I speared an apple slice with a tooth-pick and brought it to Alicia's lips.

"Mm, it's so sweet."

"It's great that you're honest."

"Did you say I was cute and honest?"

"Hang on, I'll go get you an ear pick."

"Aren't you being a little too harsh with somebody who's injured?"

"If you can joke around, you're doing just fine."

After that brief back-and-forth, we both cracked up a little. The same sort of conversation as usual. The same smiles.

"Actually, Kimizuka, how did you find that place so fast?"

Slowly, Alicia sat up, and I sat down on the little round stool beside the bed.

"Oh, I'd tagged you with a transmitter."

"Oh, I see."

"Want some more apple?"

"Yes. Ah, I'll eat my own, though." Alicia picked up one of the remaining apple pieces, put it in her mouth, and... "...Bfft! Wait, did you think you could slip that past me?!"

"Don't spit out your food." Using a tissue, I wiped off the substance that had spattered my face. It smelled awful.

"What transmitter?! That's scary! Stalker!" Alicia was hugging her shoulders, her eyes teary.

"No, you've got the wrong idea. You know how you always run off? It was a precaution."

"Seriously, when did you do that?! Where did you put it?!"

"Alicia, your underwear is surprisingly loud."

"You're awful! Of all the places I can think of, that's the very worst one!" Alicia covered her face and flopped over onto her side.

"That's why I managed to rescue you today, though."

"...That's not going to get you off the hook."

"I'm sorry, all right?"

Alicia pouted, sulking, and I stuck a piece of the small apple between her lips.

"So, what were you doing? It's really late," I said, gazing absently at the window of the hospital room.

"...I didn't want anyone else to go through anything that sad."

She was probably talking about the fifth victim's mother. Earlier, Alicia had saved the woman in a way neither Siesta nor I would have been able to.

"Besides, that's my job," she added.

"...Why are you so determined, Alicia?"

Why was she so set on becoming a detective? It wasn't as if she was obligated to do it, and neither of us was forcing her.

Besides, Alicia should have been primarily focusing on reclaiming her memory. And yet she'd prioritized the role of detective that Siesta had assigned to her, not only during this Jack the Devil incident, but even back at the beginning... Even after Siesta had tried to stop her. What on earth was driving her?

"I...," Alicia said softly. "I was always in a dark room somewhere. It was so, so dark... No light, no sound. Nothing."

That was... But no, her memory probably hadn't come back. This was just what it had felt like, a subjective impression, and that was why it was the most important factor to her.

"I didn't know anything. I was nobody. Every day, all I could do was count down until it ended. It was so boring, so painful. But then..." Alicia went on. "One day, all of a sudden, I could see. Light streamed in, I heard sounds... And then I learned how sweet apples tasted."

Alicia looked at the warped, peeled fruit on the plate and smiled faintly.

"So I thought maybe, just maybe, I could live my life over. A single thread had been lowered into that bottomless blackness. So I desperately reeled it in. I pulled and pulled... If I reached the end, if I could become someone new...if 'detective' was the mission I was assigned, then I'd live for that," Alicia told me, her expression fearless. "That's why."

She really didn't look seven, or thirteen. She looked like a woman, noble and beautiful enough to give Siesta a run for her money.

"...I'm getting a little tired."

However, that lasted for only a moment. Alicia's wan smile was as childlike as she usually was.

"I guess we chatted a bit too much."

"Uh-huh... I'm kind of sleepy."

"Well, it is the middle of the night."

Rubbing her eyes, Alicia rustled her way back under the covers.

"I'll stay here until morning, so just relax and sleep."

"Then…" Alicia slipped her left hand out from under the blankets. That ring was still on her finger. "Hold my hand."

I tried to see her face as she said that, but unfortunately, she'd solidly blocked my view with her comforter.

"Are you sure? I'll make fun of you for acting like a kid."

"…I don't care if you make fun of me. Just hold it." Her voice was sulky, but somehow persuasive.

"If those are your orders, ace detective."

I dimmed the lights, took Alicia's small left hand—and for just a little while, I slept, too.

Barely an hour later, I regretted my foolishness.

By the time the breeze from the window woke me, Alicia had vanished.

◆ That's why I wasn't qualified to pat that head

I ran through the dark streets.

Fortunately, I knew where she was now. I was headed straight for the location on my phone.

"Near here, huh?"

Finally reaching my destination, I looked around. There wasn't a soul in sight.

Then I stepped into *a certain church* with a distinctive, towering steeple.

"I can't see a thing…"

At this hour, of course, none of the lights were on. I headed into the depths, navigating by the glow of my smartphone.

Then I entered the sanctuary, where I could sense a faint light. It was coming from the moon, its beams filtering through the stained glass windows and faintly illuminating my surroundings.

I have to find Alicia, fast, I thought. I took a step forward, and just then—

I sensed something.

It wasn't close yet—but that thought didn't last long. It was on me in an instant. I couldn't fight when it was this dark. If my opponent had been hiding in here for a while, their eyes would already have adjusted. The enemy had the advantage.

"Is that what you thought?" I shifted my eye patch to the right. *My left eye was already used to the dark.* Then I aimed my gun at the figure right in front of me.

"—I surrender."

Caught off guard by my unexpected counterstrike, my opponent meekly raised both hands.

"I never thought I'd see the day when I raised the white flag to you. I may have gotten a little rusty."

"Why don't you just be happy about how much your assistant's grown—Siesta?"

We traded verbal jabs, then shrugged at each other.

I lowered the gun, shifting my eye patch back to its former position. My right eye had pretty much adjusted by now.

"What were you doing here, Kimi?"

"I could ask you the same thing. Why are you here?" I'd told her to go back home and sleep.

"I'm clearing the place out. I guessed Hel might come here, so I had them evacuate the children."

…Ah, right. The clergymen weren't the only ones at this church. There were a lot of orphans as well. This was the church that had taken Alicia in.

"What made you think Hel would come here?"

"Hmm? You ask some very odd questions." Siesta tilted her head; her expression was the same as always. "I came here because I wanted to ask you that exact same thing."

"I have several complaints about all of this, but first off, how did you know where I was? Don't tell me you tagged me with a transmitter or something."

"You must be joking. I'm not you, all right? It's instinct, born from long years," Siesta replied lightly. Personally, I found that much scarier than the alternative.

"Okay, so, next…"

"Listen."

Just as I was getting a new retort ready…

"How long do you plan to keep postponing it?"

Siesta's blue eyes were gazing at me.

She wasn't angry—she just seemed sad, or maybe resigned.

If I had to say, it was the same expression she'd worn a few days ago, when we'd fought.

"You've already realized it, too, haven't you, Kimi?"

Realized what? I cocked my head, forcing a smile.

I swear, she never just comes out and says it. Or what? Was she secretly trying to get some sort of information out of me by asking leading questions?

"Jack the Devil is looking for her lost heart. And she's *only* going after hearts."

That's right. That's why every victim up through the fifth had had their heart taken out, and why the police officer had very nearly become a victim today.

"Exactly. That police officer was wounded on the left side of his chest. Without his protective gear, he might have died. He was definitely attacked by Hel. However...in that case, what about her?"

The moonlight illuminated Siesta. Her blue eyes were still focused on me.

"Why was Alicia's right shoulder wounded? *Why did the police officer shoot her?*"

Right, come to think of it, I seemed to remember the doctor saying something about how Alicia was bleeding after getting grazed by a bullet.

But so what? Was that a problem?

I didn't get it. I didn't really understand.

More important, I needed to find Alicia. I knew she was around here somewhere.

"Don't you think he fired that shot in self-defense?"

"Siesta, move, okay? I'm..."

I put a hand on Siesta's shoulder and pushed her away, advancing across the sanctuary's red carpet.

"And didn't the knife that was on the ground with the gun seem familiar to you?"

I didn't know. I knew nothing about that. I hadn't checked to see whether the knife from the crime scene *resembled the knife that had disappeared from our kitchen.*

"Assistant, listen."

"—Never mind that, we have to find Alicia, fast!"

I had to hurry and get out of here. I had to go somewhere Siesta's words couldn't reach me, or else...!

"I know you knew, too, Kimi."

The sorrow in her voice was too much for me, and I turned back.

Behind Siesta, at the back of the inner sanctum, the Virgin Mary was watching me.

"I mean, the real reason *you put a tracker in that ring* was—"

"Stop!"

My scream echoed pathetically in the vast church.

Yeah, I know. I know.

I'd realized a long time ago that Hel and Alicia were the same person.

◆ Once again, we leave on a journey

I'd suspected that Hel, or "Jack the Devil," was actually Alicia, and yet until the very, very end, I'd behaved as though I still had at least a tiny shred of belief in her. Had that been because of her mind control ability, or had I personally wanted to trust her? I didn't know.

The only certainty was that Alicia had been our enemy.

"...But Siesta."

Even now, I was trying to struggle against that incontrovertible fact.

"If Hel and Alicia are the same person, then what about the fake Ms. Fuubi? Didn't you say that was Hel at first?"

Alicia had been there during that visit. If that fake had been Hel, then Alicia had to be unrelated to this after all, and—

"No, Alicia was Hel; she'd used Cerberus's ability to transform herself. We should assume that that fake was yet *another enemy*."

"No... You're saying we're up against two shapeshifters?"

"That's probably the most reasonable theory. *That one* may even be the more troublesome foe. Such as their *boss,* for example."

...! It couldn't be. SPES had worse opponents than Hel?

"Right now, though, *Hel* takes priority. We have to find her fast, or..."

"You mean *Alicia!*" As Siesta began to turn, I caught her hand. "Not Hel, Alicia. She's… She's…"

I knew. I knew, I knew. Logically anyway. But my heart hadn't caught up. I still didn't want to admit it.

"During our fight, Hel's heart was wounded. Immediately afterward, Jack the Devil began stealing human hearts, and right at the same time, an unidentified girl appeared on our doorstep. Listen, Assistant." Siesta turned back to me. "Are you saying all of that is one big coincidence?"

I let go of her hand.

"…Did you know the whole time?"

"No. If I'd realized it sooner, there would have been fewer victims… But I just couldn't bring myself to suspect her until the last minute."

It probably had been her ability, then. Siesta never let her personal feelings affect what she did. When we'd looked into Hel's—into Alicia's—eyes, and listened to what she said, we'd become absolutely incapable of doubting her.

It was mind control. Both Siesta and I had been in the palm of Alicia's hand the whole time.

"That can't be right." The quiet echo of my voice sounded pitiful in the church. "Then what? You're saying that smile of hers, and her tears, her kindness, every little thing, was just a misunderstanding?"

What about her scream?

Those words that had saved the fifth victim's mother—had they been a lie, too?

"No, I think those were genuine."

That was some small consolation.

"Alicia's encouragement really did help her. She told us it was almost as if her own daughter was speaking to her, remember?"

Yeah. She'd said it with tears on her face. She'd hugged Alicia to her, and—

"…!" I broke out in goose bumps all over, and a choked noise escaped me.

"Back then, Alicia had…"

The heart of that woman's daughter inside her chest.

The mother had embraced the murderer who'd killed her own child as if that murderer were the daughter herself.

That was just… There was no fixing this.

We had to find Alicia quickly, quickly. We had to stop her, or else…

"I'm sorry. I fail as an ace detective, don't I?"

We hadn't even had to look for her: She came to us voluntarily.

Alicia was standing in the door of the church with a sad smile.

…But as a matter of fact, we'd known she was going to come here.

After Hel had lost her heart during that fight, she'd searched for a new one. She'd gone through five hearts, one after another, and had failed to take a sixth one earlier. She had to get a fresh heart as fast as she could—and she'd come to the church because she knew that, even at this hour, she would find people here. She'd been targeting the heart of one of the other orphans. One who should have been her companion.

"Alicia…"

She was coming closer and closer, and I couldn't move.

Yet I didn't sense any hostility from her. Siesta and I were standing side by side, and Alicia stopped in front of us.

"There's another me inside me, I think." Alicia set her hand over the left side of her chest. "Of the two of us, I'm sure I'm the 'shadow' side. I think that's why I don't have any memories, why I don't know who I am, and why I was always in the dark."

Dissociative identity disorder, sometimes known as having multiple personalities.

It was a type of defensive reaction. When someone went through pain or suffering too great for their mind to bear, they severed those memories and emotions from themselves and integrated them as a different personality, to reduce their physical and mental burden.

For example, abuse inflicted by parents in childhood resulted in trauma, and in an effort to lessen the emotional damage, the child created another personality. A considerable number of cases like that had been reported, from countries all over the world.

In this case, we could conjecture that Hel was the main personality, the one who'd existed first. During that battle, she'd sustained major damage; her mind had dissociated from the event, and Alicia's personality had surfaced. That was why Alicia hadn't known who she was, and why she'd had hardly any memories.

"I did keep telling you, remember? I'm really seventeen." Alicia cracked a rather strained-sounding joke.

"...Yeah, you did. Sorry for not believing you."

Alicia's appearance was probably something temporary that Hel had created using Cerberus's ability. The real Alicia was seventeen, and her true form was that red-eyed girl in the military uniform.

"I think even I'd realized it, really," Alicia murmured suddenly. "I just pretended I hadn't, the whole time."

"...Noticed what?"

"That the other me was killing people while I was unconscious." Alicia clutched at her own chest, squeezing her hand into a fist. "It's so strange, though. When I was investigating with Kimizuka, I thought maybe the culprit really was someone else. I really, really wanted it to be true."

In that hospital bed, Alicia had told me about it—how she'd been in darkness for a long time, and how, all of a sudden, light had streamed in. How beyond it was a new self, and a new role, that she'd tried to hold on to. A swarm of hands had reached out for her from the pit of hell, and Alicia had fled from them as best she could.

"Alicia, it's not your fault." I gripped her shoulders. "Even if your hands killed people, *you yourself haven't done anything!*"

I mean, it was true, wasn't it? Alicia hadn't done anything bad.

True, she was a little selfish, and she wasn't exactly eager to do what she was told, and being with her had given me a lot of trouble—but she was kind, too. She could share others' joy. She could have fun with them. She could get angry for their sake and cry for them.

That wasn't a misunderstanding or anything like it. No one had *made me think it.* These were just the impressions I'd built over those few weeks with her. I'd never let this disaster break them! This wasn't Alicia's fault. She hadn't done a thing... Not one thing...

"Kimizuka, I'm sorry. I guess I was *still a bad kid* after all." Alicia was crying.

She bit her lip while round, jewellike tears fell from her large eyes.

"We never needed to go out and hunt for a devil, did we."

One of those tears fell onto the ring finger of her left hand.

"The devil was inside me all along."

Alicia's ring cracked audibly.

The blue jewel shattered, and the transmitter I'd hidden in it flew apart in fragments.

"Assistant!"

Siesta shoved me out of the way, and I crashed into the ground. When I hastily looked up, Alicia's left arm was frozen mid-swing. She was holding a knife, and Siesta had put her arms up, catching it with a cross block.

She was holding the fruit knife I'd used to peel the apple in her hospital room.

"Alicia..."

Her eyes were blank—she was in a trance. Alicia's mind wasn't there anymore. Was this how she'd attacked those five people? ...But even if she could overpower ordinary civilians, she was no match for Siesta.

"I'm sorry."

Apologizing quietly, Siesta pinned Alicia to the floor and pushed the muzzle of a Magnum against the back of her skull.

"Siesta, don't!" The next thing I knew, I'd shoved her out of the way.

"Are you stupid, Kimi?! If we don't do this here—!"

"No, you can't! If you solve this by killing her, Alicia won't... She won't...!"

"Can't you tell those emotions are going to skew vital decisions?!"

"Didn't you just learn that's how people are?!"

Siesta and I each trained our guns on the other's forehead.

For both of us, this was our line in the sand. We couldn't compromise.

"Well, well. Infighting?"

I heard a voice from somewhere. I searched for it but couldn't locate it... But we'd been through a similar experience a few weeks back.

"Allow me to reclaim her."

In that instant, Alicia's prone body abruptly vanished.

"...! Chameleon!"

I glared into empty space. Even if I couldn't see him, I knew he had to be there.

"I've had quite a time searching for her, you know. I took my eye off her for one moment, and then she was gone. Not only did she change her shape, but she'd even lost her memory."

...So it was true, then. After that first battle, Hel had used Cerberus's ability to change into this form in order to hide from us. However, she'd taken a lot of damage both mentally and physically, and Alicia's personality had accidentally surfaced. She'd been wandering the streets of London— And that must have been when I'd found her, asleep in that cardboard box.

"It seems she will require full-scale *treatment*. For now, I will take her back to *my abode*."

"—Where are you going?!"

"In the ocean approximately seven hundred nautical miles to the northwest, there is an isolated island that serves as our stronghold. What do you say? I believe it is about time, is it not? Once you've prepared yourselves, why not come for a visit?"

In a meticulously polite tone, Chameleon issued his declaration of war.

"Now then. We shall be waiting."

That was the last thing he said, and then he was truly gone.

The only ones left were Siesta and me.

A hollow, heavy silence fell.

I'd lost a companion, and the bond I'd spent that time cultivating. I couldn't even look Siesta in the eye.

After a few minutes, or maybe half an hour or more...

"...—!"

A sharp pain ran through my back.

"...I thought you'd shot me."

When I twisted around from where I was sitting on the ground, Siesta had just finished whacking me on the back, hard.

"Are you stupid, Kimi?"

Yeah, that's fine. You can call me as many names as you want. But—

"I'm not apologizing."

Instead of looking at Siesta, I let my back do the talking.

"That's all right. You don't have to." To my surprise, Siesta sat down on the spot, back to back with me. "You were trying to do what was right, and so was I. So you don't have to apologize. I won't either. That's just fine for us," Siesta said, behind me.

"...What should we do now?" I asked pathetically. We'd lost everything.

In response, Siesta said...

"First, let's go to the store together."

She was perfectly calm, speaking to me in the same tone she always used.

"Let's buy the biggest, reddest, roundest apples we can find. Then we'll make a delicious apple pie, and eat it, and brew some truly exceptional tea and drink it together. After that, well...if you insist, we can take a bath together... Although I will be wearing a bath towel, mind you. Then, when night comes, we could order pizza, and drink a toast with cola, and watch rented movies all night long. We'll fall asleep in the middle of one of them, and we'll both be cranky when we wake up, and we'll fight over petty things. Then we'll spend the day the way we always do, and after that—"

The heat on my back disappeared, and I turned around.

My partner was standing there, holding out her hand to me to pull me up from the floor.

"Let's set off on a journey to save our friend."

I took her hand without hesitating.

Maybe then the three of us could walk together again, one more time.

Chapter 4

◆ An ark of hope, bound for the end

"Then Alicia is probably at that laboratory, or whatever it is?"

In a small boat that was sailing over a rough ocean, I checked our game plan with Siesta again.

"Yes, that's right. It sounds as if she's trying to recover physically there," Siesta answered with a nod, taking a sip of black tea from her favorite cup.

The boat had been rocking violently for a while now, but she was elegantly enjoying her teatime and hadn't spilled a drop. Considering the importance of the mission we were about to tackle, it couldn't have been easy to act so laidback...but that was common sense, and the ace detective was anything but commonsensical.

It had been five days since the tragedy at the church.

We were on our way to a certain remote island that was under the effective control of SPES.

Our goal was clear: subdue Hel and reclaim Alicia.

Problem was, those two were the same person.

Defeat Hel and rescue Alicia—was there a way to resolve that contradiction? I didn't know. However...

"It's all right. I have a plan," Siesta said calmly, as if to clear away my unease.

She hadn't told Charlie and me what the specific maneuver was, but that was how she always worked. Over the past three years, we'd gotten along like that just fine. I was sure that this time would be the same, so—

"I want you and Charlie to make for the laboratory."

"Me and Charlie, huh...? Well, okay—for now—but what are you going to do, Siesta?"

"I'll investigate this area. According to the intel, there's something like a military maneuver range here."

Siesta unrolled a piece of paper that seemed to be a faded map.

Apparently, she'd gotten this information out of Bat, who was back in Japan. The guy had originally been our enemy—and of course he still was, but he still lent us a hand at times like this. He'd probably been charmed by the ace detective. Either way, this time, he'd completely saved our butts.

"Just wait, Alicia."

Alicia, or Hel, was somewhere on this island. Had she finished the treatment Chameleon had mentioned, or was she still unconscious? Either way, we had to find her ASAP.

"Haaah. I'd rather go with you, Ma'am." Charlie puffed her cheeks out like a little kid.

We'd had a bit of a scene over this particular problem a little while ago, but I'd thought we'd worked it out…

"Hmm. I'd worry about leaving my assistant on his own, you see."

Siesta reasoned with Charlie in a motherly way—but she didn't have to directly imply that I wasn't reliable. Harsh.

"Ma'am, will you really be all right on your own?" Charlie's eyes wavered uncertainly. She was probably worried that Hel might have completed her treatment and regained her strength and personality. As a matter of fact, when we'd first fought Hel in London, she'd very nearly put Siesta's back against the wall.

But…

"It's fine." Siesta gave Charlie a serene smile. "Hel's heart probably isn't functioning right now."

After being defeated by Siesta, Hel had stolen five people's hearts as Jack the Devil. Why had she taken so many new hearts in rapid succession? Probably because they hadn't been compatible with her body.

That was only to be expected. Organ donations couldn't come from just anyone. This case was special, since Hel was a pseudohuman.

Right now, Hel was burning through new hearts like batteries, one after another. She'd used up her fifth and had been about to try for a sixth when Siesta and I had found her.

Meaning that right now, Hel's body only had that fifth heart, and it was very nearly worn out. If she was that weak, Siesta would be able to beat

her. Then, if there was a way to rescue Alicia's consciousness on its own…
No, Siesta must have come up with a plan for that already.

"So this is finally it, hmm?"

It had been a month since we'd met Hel and Alicia.

Three years since I'd started fighting SPES.

This long journey was finally nearing its end. That thought made me stand straighter, whether I wanted to or not.

"Are you nervous?" Siesta asked as she set down her teacup.

"Excited. These are warrior shakes."

"Oh, you really are trembling."

"In a good way, though, all right?"

"Pfft!"

"Charlie, you shut up."

"Assistant, shall I stroke your head?"

"Ma'am, I'm scared…"

"You're a serious bootlicker, you know that?"

Charlie ran up to Siesta's knees. I'd already seen this happen way too often.

"You're sure you're fine, Kimi?" asked Siesta, tilting her head as she stroked Charlie's blond hair.

"Don't be dumb. I'm not gonna embarrass myself like that."

There was no way I could act so laidback right before we went into the final battle.

"…Hmph."

Although there was no telling what she was thinking, Charlie raised her head from Siesta's lap. "I'll let you have my spot."

No, you totally don't need to. Even if you set me up, I can't—

"Come on, then." Siesta spread her arms wide, and the corners of her lips rose slightly.

"…That's a pretty exaggerated pose for stroking somebody's head."

"I thought I'd take the opportunity to hug you."

Look, I told you, we're supposed to be bracing for the battle.

…No, maybe that's why she was doing it: because I was tense. Still, nobody asked for that.

"Hmm? You aren't coming to me."

"If you wanna press your boobs against guys, at least have some shame about it."

"You do use unique expressions. Well, never mind," Siesta said, lowering her arms. "Some other time, then."

"Specifically, never."

After that exchange, we laughed a little. We were fine the way we were, Siesta and I.

"Looks like it's almost time."

Siesta squinted out over the sea, at the final destination of our three-year journey.

◆ With the sound of the engine and the wind in my ears

Very soon, we reached the island's port (which was practically just the shoreline) and disembarked, unloading our cargo.

"All right, we'll be back."

"Please do be careful, Ma'am."

Charlie exchanged a firm handshake with Siesta, and I...caved to Siesta's wordless pressure and gave a light smack of a high five.

"See you later."

Then we threw ourselves into our final mission.

"The wind feels good," I commented. Even with everything else going on, the sensation was so nice, I had to say something.

The faint scent of the ocean drifted in the air.

"So to get to the research facility, we just have to go straight this way, right?" Charlie asked, speaking louder than usual.

"Yeah, from what I saw of the map, that should do it." I raised my voice a little, too.

That was because we were currently riding double on a motorcycle toward our destination.

The bike was big enough that it had only barely fit on the boat, but we'd needed it to execute the maneuver smoothly. This island was SPES's den; we couldn't afford to take our time here.

"...Actually, shouldn't this be the other way around?" Charlie, who wasn't wearing a helmet, shot a glance back at me.

"What's the other way around?"

"Our positions!" she snapped.

That's weird. I'm pretty sure I'm not doing anything wrong.

"Ordinarily, driving is the guy's job for these things, isn't it?!"

Ah. Apparently she was unhappy about the fact that we were riding double, and I'd left the driving to her.

"Well, I don't have a license."

"God, you're pathetic!"

"You've lived in America; it's not a fair comparison."

It's the law. The laws are different, okay?

"...Also."

"Also what?"

"D-don't hold on so hard," she complained, darting another look back at me.

"I mean, it's scary."

"Riding double on a motorbike scares you? You're a guy, aren't you?"

"Hugging your waist just makes me feel very secure."

"If you wanted to sexually harass me, that was the worst attempt in the history of the world."

While that pointless conversation was happening, we were racing down a natural trail.

A wide plain rolled away in all directions, with no sign of people anywhere. However, I could see a row of white wind lenses in the distance. The fact that there was an energy supply made it clear that there was human civilization here.

"Back there," Charlie began without decelerating, "you should have let Ma'am hug you." She laughed. "If you want to hold on to girls so badly."

"Moron. You think I could do anything that pathetic?"

"You're currently doing something exactly that pathetic."

"It's more that I don't care what you think of me, Charlie."

"I'm gonna throw you off this bike," Charlie retorted. "...Although I'd fall off, too."

Then maybe don't keep jerking the handlebars around? Quit it; you are actually going to kill me.

"You'll regret it, though. If you're always so stubborn..." Charlie suddenly admonished me. "Ma'am is all you have, after all."

Siesta is all I have?

That's not true— I tried to argue, but the words wouldn't come out how I wanted.

If Siesta went away...

I tried to think about that "if"...then stopped. I didn't have to consider that particular possibility today, did I?

Right now, I should just concentrate on the mission we were about to perform.

"But it's not like it goes both ways."

...And so I tried to evade her words with nonsense like that.

"Siesta has you, Charlie. And her other allies, of course. It's not like I'm her one-and-only anything..."

"No, she doesn't," Charlie said. Her voice was vaguely melancholy. "You're all she has, too."

I didn't know how to respond to that, so I just listened to the engine and the wind.

◆ SPES

Before long, we reached the laboratory. It was dark inside, and we tried to proceed as quickly and carefully as we could.

We didn't have a map of the facility itself, so we had to make our way through it by feel. It wasn't clear whether Alicia—or Hel—was here at all; if our search didn't turn up anything after a while, we'd need to hurry back and rendezvous with Siesta.

"Nobody's...here."

We'd gone down a flight of stairs, and Charlie glanced around.

"Yeah. I figured we'd have to fight two or three battles at the very least." But if we'd managed to get in here this easily... Was it a dead end?

If so, it was very likely that Siesta had drawn the lucky number.

"Kimizuka." Charlie tugged on my cuff. "Over there." She was pointing at a freight elevator. When we approached, it seemed to be in working order.

"Wanna give it a shot?" Charlie nodded, and we rode it down to the basement. When the elevator doors opened, the sight that met us was—

"...! What is...?"

A sea of blood.

The floor was littered with corpses that had been so badly mutilated, I wanted to cover my eyes.

"Ngh..."

Even Charlie, who should have been used to scenes like this, clapped a hand over her mouth. It was horrible.

But that didn't mean we could turn around and leave. A man was standing there, like the king of that mountain of corpses.

"Are you Cerberus...?"

The sturdy, middle-aged man wearing a black robe looked exactly like the Cerberus I'd fought a month ago.

"...No, that can't be."

I'd confirmed it with Siesta several times. Cerberus had been killed, right in front of us—by Hel. In which case...

"Are you thinking I am Hel, who has inherited Cerberus's ability and used it to take his shape?" The man had virtually read my mind. "Unfortunately, you are wrong. I am neither Cerberus nor Hel."

The man's figure warped, then stabilized in the shape of—

"Ha-hah. Remember this one?"

"...! Bat...!"

"Hey, yeah. I like that reaction." He was talking like Bat now; with both this form and Cerberus, it was like speaking to the real deal.

"—Then who are you?!"

Charlie drew her gun, pointing it at the man.

That's what I wanted to know. He could camouflage himself as Cerberus and Bat, but who was this guy anyway?

"Their parent."

The man was still wearing Bat's shape, but this time he responded in what was probably his own persona.

"Parent...? You mean Cerberus's, or Bat's?"

"Both of them." He surveyed the pile of corpses with those clouded emerald eyes.

"...! Then— No, you can't mean..."

The gun in Charlie's hands wavered slightly.

This masterful transformation ability. There was no doubt about it: This man was the true identity of the counterfeit Ms. Fuubi who'd visited Siesta, Alicia, and me earlier. And as Siesta had said—that counterfeit just might be the head of SPES.

"We run into this thing the one time Siesta's not here? Man, talk about shitty luck…"

I guess it was par for the course for me. That's exactly what my knack for getting dragged into things does. I had to laugh at myself—or I'd never manage to stop shaking.

"What, it's okay for a parent to kill their kids?"

Taking a cue from Charlie, I pointed my gun at the enemy boss, a few meters away.

"What are you saying? My status as a parent is what gives me permission to kill my children."

…—! This was awful. The guy was as hard to reach as Hel, maybe even worse. Actually, I didn't want to be talking to him at all.

"These are all my children. Offspring I bore. Thus, I am free to do as I please with them. Am I wrong?"

The false Bat cocked his head, as if he really didn't see the problem in what he was saying.

"When'd I stumble into the world where men are the main childbearers?" I cracked a joke, buying time as I desperately tried to think of what we should do next— But…

"Do you intend to place me in your human categories of male or female?"

"What, are you saying you're a monster instead?"

"No."

At that, our greatest enemy, the foe we had to defeat, told us directly what he was.

"I am *a plant*."

At that sudden bombshell, Charlie and I exchanged looks—but all we saw was bewilderment.

What the hell was this guy saying?

A plant? Had he just called himself a plant?

"Of course, that's only in relation to the classifications with which you are familiar. However, I am neither human nor monster. I am Seed, a plant who flew to this world from the depths of space."

Whoa, whoa, when did this story go intergalactic?

A plant from outer space? An invader?

Gimme a break… What on earth have we been fighting all this time?

"…Then you're saying the other pseudohumans are actually plants, too?"

"'Pseudohuman' is just the name you chose to give them. Both I and they have only ever been plants. Here, you've seen these before, haven't you?"

The next moment, a long, wriggling, tentacle-like thing sprouted from Seed's right ear, exactly like the one Bat had on the plane three years ago. But now, what I'd thought was a tentacle *also looked like the thick root of a plant.*

"—What are you people trying to do? Why is SPES committing terrorist attacks?" Charlie interrogated Seed, careful to keep her gun aimed at his root while she spoke.

SPES: the secret organization Siesta had been pursuing, all this time. She'd said its name meant "hope" in Latin. But these guys had been sowing nothing but despair. They believed in some screwy book called the "sacred text," committed acts of terror, and killed innocent people.

"Answer us, Seed. Is it world domination? Immortality? A desire for knowledge? It can't be just the impulse to destroy stuff, can it? Or are you planning to claim it's your mission, the way Hel did? Come on, what exactly are you trying to accomplish here? If you're a plant who came from some other planet, what do you intend to do here on Earth?"

Come on, bring it. I just listed all the evil motives I can think of. But I don't care what answer you give me; I'm going to fire back with sound arguments and bullets. With newfound resolve, I squeezed the grip of my gun even tighter.

"It's in order to survive."

For a moment, that perfectly straightforward answer took the wind out of my sails, and I almost dropped the gun.

"…To survive?"

"Yes. We have only one goal."

There was no telling what he was thinking as Seed used the root that had sprouted from his ear to lop off his own right arm. Still, he kept talking.

"Surface of the Planet Exploding Seeds— We will cover this world with our seeds."

◆ A true fiend

"That is the true meaning of SPES, and our real objective."

As I stood there, stunned, the guy's right arm began to regenerate from the wound in the blink of an eye, while a new body began to form from the severed arm on the ground. It wasn't fully human-shaped, but it was rapidly acquiring all the bumps and hollows of a body.

"It's like a cutting…"

"Yes. Exactly." Charlie nodded.

"Charlie, I can still tell you don't understand."

"…Well, I thought I'd lighten the mood. It was getting too serious, you know?"

Don't lie. Everybody already knows you're kinda dumb.

"A cutting is when you clip a stalk off the parent plant, put it in the ground so it sprouts roots, and grow another plant from it. Basically—"

"It's a plant…clone?"

Exactly. That was what Seed had meant when he'd called himself a parent. All the members of SPES were his clones. Seed was the original pseudohuman.

That was why he could take on Cerberus's and Bat's forms, and why he could use their powers. It was actually the other way around—Seed had shared his abilities with them.

"I am a plant that reached this world by accident—a 'primordial seed,' as it were. The most fundamental desire of all living things, plant or animal, is to leave descendants. I create clones from my own body, as I've demonstrated, then sow them across the planet's surface in the hopes that they will find prosperity."

"...Do you think that makes it okay to kill people who've done nothing wrong?"

"What problem could there be with eliminating an invasive species that obstructs the spread of my seeds?"

"—*You're* the invasive species!" My finger pulled the trigger and fired at the root that had grown from Seed—but it was a no-go.

"Even minutes after its birth, its instinct to protect its parent seems to be functioning."

The newborn pseudohuman from Seed's severed right arm still looked like a mud doll, but it had unsteadily gotten to its feet and shielded him from the bullet. It crumpled to the ground, as if its strings had been cut.

"...Doesn't that make you feel sad at all?" I took in the sight of Seed's comrades, who lay around him. He'd said he hoped for the prosperity of his seeds, but what he was doing was the exact opposite.

"These were necessary sacrifices, to ensure the continued existence of my seeds. Don't worry; their *seeds* haven't been wasted."

As he spoke, Seed took an object like a small, jet-black rock from the clone that had just collapsed. It was the same as the thing Hel had removed from Cerberus's chest earlier.

"A seed...? You mean that rock?"

If I remembered right, Siesta had said those things were like cores that created pseudohumans. When Seed had called himself "the primordial seed," was that what he'd meant?

"That's right. Some of the seeds of our departed comrades have been inherited by *her*."

"...! You mean Hel...?"

That must have been the "treatment" Chameleon had mentioned. So they'd transplanted seeds from Hel's comrades into her? No wonder we hadn't passed a single soul on our way here.

"Where is Hel now?"

From what I'd heard, Hel's personality was probably in charge now. In that case, we had to find a way to defeat her and rescue Alicia as quickly as possible.

"As she isn't here, there is only one place where she would conceivably be, correct?"

...! *With Siesta?!*

"Kimizuka! Ma'am is—!"

"Yeah, I know. Let's hurry."

Then, just as we'd turned to go—

"Do you imagine escaping will be that simple?"

I heard a familiar, unpleasantly polite voice from some untraceable location.

"Chameleon…!"

The very guy who'd taken Alicia from right under our noses. He was probably using his ability to make himself invisible, but he was definitely in the room with us right now.

"Ha-ha. It appears as though I'll be able to entertain myself here as well."

Here as well? Don't tell me…

"Kimizuka!"

Keeping her gun trained on empty space, Charlie signaled at me with her eyes.

"Yeah, I know."

Chameleon was talking as if he'd already fought a battle somewhere—meaning he had to have fought Siesta while she was off on her own mission. But Chameleon was here now, which meant… It couldn't mean… But would Siesta lose to a guy like him?

No, wait. Of course. If he'd been with Hel, who was back to her old self, then—

"Kimizuka, let me handle this." Charlie urged me to go to Siesta. "I'll hold them here. Hurry—"

"I would prefer not to be ignored."

Chameleon's voice sounded as if it was moving all over the place. Not only could we not finish him off, but there was no telling when an attack would come flying at us. It was about ten meters to the door. How was I going to get that far—?

"You've interrupted your parent."

And then, Seed vanished.

"Ghaaaaaaaaaaaaaaaaaaaaaah!"

The next thing we heard was Chameleon's scream.

For the first time, I got a clear look at him. He had silver hair and rather bland Asian features. Seed had his right hand clamped around his neck and was holding him suspended in midair.

"I was talking just now. Why did you break in?"

"...I'm...v-very...sorry..."

Chameleon barely managed to get the words out. A colored fluid was welling from his mouth.

"I am only letting you live so you can guard *that*. Don't forget yourself," Seed hissed, then slammed Chameleon into the floor.

He wouldn't have done it to protect us. He'd only been punishing the guy for disrespecting his parent. However—

"Seed, why did you give us so much information about SPES?"

What were you even doing here? Why did you stay after you massacred your comrades in order to keep Hel alive? If you're SPES's commander-in-chief, wouldn't you normally be the one to go defeat Siesta?

In response to those natural questions, Seed said...

"Because if I side with either of them, the plan won't come together."

With that enigmatic reply, he blinked out of sight.

"Of course he can use Chameleon's abilities too, huh...?"

Where had he gone, though? I could only hope that it wasn't wherever Siesta was.

"Kimizuka, go now." Charlie pointed her gun at Chameleon, who'd collapsed on the floor, and urged me to leave.

"Damn... Dammit...!"

However, Chameleon shakily got to his feet, clearly in agony. He cloaked himself again and attacked us from all sides. We couldn't even see his shadow.

"I'm sick of watching this same move over and over." Charlie fired *at empty space*.

"...Ghk! You have fine instincts," I heard Chameleon say. Had that random shot grazed him?

"Instincts? Huh. You tell funny jokes for a reptile," Charlie retorted.

Urging me to go with a glance, she squeezed the trigger again. "The stench of your breath makes you obvious."

If a girl said that to me, I'd never recover. Smiling wryly, I broke into a run, leaving the rest to Charlie, but then—

"Kimizuka!"

Something flew through the air, and I caught it in my right hand. When I opened my fingers, it turned out to be a key.

I already told her I don't have a license.

"Let me ride behind you someday."

"...Yeah, I'll practice."

And if I crash your beloved bike today...cut a guy some slack, all right?

◆ If we meet again, away from this island

After that, I hopped on Charlie's bike and headed for the opposite side of the island, gunning the engine the whole way. There were no civilians here and no need to obey traffic laws, so it didn't matter if I'd never driven before. I just gripped the handlebars and thought only of getting to Siesta as fast as I possibly could.

I couldn't believe Siesta would lose to a guy on Chameleon's level. But if Hel was with him, fully revived, then just maybe...

"...Dammit."

My thoughts went in the worst possible directions.

But if something happened to Siesta, Charlie and I would be no match for Hel, which meant Alicia's rescue would fail as well. And that meant Siesta's safety was top priority—

"...No, that's wrong."

Even if Alicia wasn't part of this at all, if Siesta was in trouble—I would have gone to help her without hesitating.

"She's trained me really well."

Praying that I'd make it in time, I roared along on Charlie's beloved bike.

"...! Siesta!"

When I found her, roughly two hours after we'd last seen each other, she was lying facedown on the ground.

Letting the bike tip over, I ran to my partner. "Siesta! Hey!" I picked up her prone body and rested her on my knees.

Her small, pale face was covered with sand. As I brushed it off with my fingertips, I called her name over and over.

"This isn't funny! You promised you wouldn't go off and die without telling me! Remember...?!"

No, this wasn't gonna work. I needed to calm down, now more than ever. Calm down and do what I could, take the steps I needed to save Siesta.

"Gimme a break, all right?"

I rolled up my sleeves, laid Siesta back down on the ground, and put my hands against her chest.

I set my right hand on top of my left one, straightened my elbows, and pushed with all my weight behind it.

"—Five centimeters."

Chest compressions don't work unless you press down that far into the rib cage. Strangely enough, this wasn't my first time performing CPR. After all, I get dragged into this stuff all the time.

I was grateful for that coincidence now as I pressed down on Siesta's chest. She'd been so strong physically, and yet her body was so delicate that it felt like I could break it with far less pressure than this.

"Don't you dare—die...!"

I kept on compressing Siesta's chest to a regular rhythm.

Ten times, twenty...thirty.

Next, I had to give her two artificial breaths. I secured her airway, pinched her nose between my fingertips, then took a deep breath.

"Forgive me."

Keeping my eyes wide open so I wouldn't miss, I leaned in toward Siesta's lips, and just then—

"I hadn't considered the possibility that you might come here."

Her blue eyes blinked open.

"...Heeeeeeeey! You stu— Y-you!" I leaned back so far that my legs gave out, and Siesta sat up.

"Hmm. Who'd have thought you'd come to me? That's a problem. You've thrown off my plan." While she was busy being confusing, she brushed the sand and dust off her dress. "Was it because your love for me was far more obsessive than I'd thought?"

"...I don't really know what's happening, but I'm going to object to that analysis anyway."

"And another thing, Kimi—performing CPR is fine, but you're generally supposed to make sure the person isn't breathing naturally first."

I was still hugging the ground, and Siesta looked down at me coldly.

"Wait, your heart was beating the whole time?"

"Well, no, it wasn't, but..."

"So it stopped?!" *Then why are you yelling at me?*

"Oh, no, no." Siesta waved a hand from side to side, dismissively. "My heart didn't stop. I stopped it."

"You...stopped it?"

I was really lost now, so for lack of anything better to do, I just took the hand she'd held out to me and got to my feet.

"Well, an enemy who was a bit of a pain picked a fight with me, so I was playing dead."

"...I've been asking you for three years: What the heck are you?"

I wasn't even surprised anymore. I was so appalled, my knees were trembling.

An enemy who was a bit of a pain... Ah, I think I get it. Chameleon must have gotten the impression that he'd killed Siesta, and felt his job was done.

"Well, 'a pain' may not be the word. I'm oddly incompatible with that one." Siesta closed one blue eye in a deliberate wink.

Still, could normal people literally play dead?

"What kind of body do you have anyway? Geez."

Smiling wryly, I was about to retaliate with a karate chop, when—

"Huh?"

—the next thing I knew, I was sitting on my butt on the ground.

"What's the matter?" she asked.

"Uh, I just sort of..."

Siesta gave me a blank look. And then...

"Did the relief make your legs give out?" she asked with a little smile. "Because I was fine?"

"—. Quit smirking. Don't let your lips wriggle like that, either."

"May I be frank about what I'm feeling right now?"

"No. Don't. Don't you dare. I'm not listening to anything you say."

"I think you're adorable, Kimi."

"Aaaaaaah! Aaaaaaaah! I can't heeeear youuuuu!"

Dammit, why did I have to take this humiliation? All this after I'd driven here full-tilt on a bike I couldn't even ride. After I'd actually attempted CPR. It was so weird. This was obviously weird...

"What should I do? Shall I stroke your head after all?"

"Absolutely not!"

"How about a hug?"

"No way in hell!"

"Or to borrow your turn of phrase, 'press my boobs against you.'"

"You can't just *do* that. I mean it. To me or any guy."

"Oh, but you already touched my chest a minute ago, didn't you?" Siesta giggled. "Thirty times, even."

"Not fair. Siesta, you're trying to kill me, aren't you? Socially."

"Heh-heh. You really are fun to tease, Kimi. —It really was fun."

"...Siesta?"

Suddenly, her smile grew slightly melancholy.

When I saw her face, I knew everything. I'd been right next to her, watching her profile, for three years. No matter how little I wanted to, I knew what had happened, and what was about to happen.

"Siesta."

"What?"

"Let me take you up on that hug after all, just once."

I stood up and turned around.

A lone girl stood there.

"If we survive and meet again, away from this island."

◆ Rematch

"So. Which one are you?" I asked the girl who'd been standing behind me.

"You'd think you could tell by looking at me."

She had red eyes, and a red military uniform. There were several sabers at her waist. She was obviously the one we'd fought to the death in London, and her name was—

"Hel..."

She wasn't Alicia. The girl who was standing here right now was Hel. The enemy we had to defeat.

"I think we can assume that the treatment's been completed—using your companions' lives," Siesta said, coming up to stand beside me. She watched Hel with stern, piercing eyes. She must have heard about that earlier, maybe from Chameleon.

"Companions? Who would those be?" Hel tilted her head, as if she genuinely didn't understand what she was hearing.

I'd seen that expression just a little while ago, when I asked Seed whether he felt guilty about killing his children.

"Do you seriously not know?"

Was that the difference between humans and plants? Did these guys give top priority to their seeds' prosperity?

"What about Chameleon, then? Even in London, you two were working together..."

"I only used him because he was a perfect cover," Hel replied casually. "I imagine he thinks the same way. Chameleon has no interest in me as an individual. To him, I'm just a symbol, a red military uniform."

...Actually, when Alicia had been the dominant personality in Hel's body, it had taken Chameleon several weeks to find her. With their sharp ears and noses, Bat and Cerberus might be different. Did these people not view each other as individuals normally?

"Unlike you people, I have no interest in playing at being comrades." Hel sneered at Siesta and me with her frosty red eyes.

"...That was a very significant way to put it." Siesta stepped in front of me, facing Hel a few meters away. "What is it that you really want to say?"

"Oh, nothing. Only that you seemed to have been on very friendly terms with her."

"Her"... She meant Alicia. That was why Hel had been talking about "playing at being comrades."

"That's right. That's why we're here to save Alicia."

"I know. That's why you're going to kill me."

The next instant, the ground bulged up, and *a tangle of thorny vines like bramble canes shot up from it.*

"Meaning I'm allowed to kill you as well, aren't I?"

The bramble whips turned on Siesta and me.

"What the heck are those?"

"It means the enemy wasn't stupid. I'm sure they've planted the entire island with their seeds." Siesta analyzed the situation for me, using a term I'd heard only a short while ago.

"...Okay. So we have to fight the whole island, huh?"

Right now, everything on this island was preparing to attack us, with their survival instincts in high gear. Quite literally, the seeds had already been sown.

And yet as she faced down the enemy of the world, the ace detective didn't even flinch.

"Actually, this is a very fitting place for our final battle."

"Isn't it? For your last moments, I mean."

Siesta's musket and Hel's red sword took aim at each other, forming a straight line.

"I'll win. And I promise I'll make Alicia's wish come true."

"No, you're going to die here. You can't save that girl."

There was a single gunshot, and the sound of a sword slicing through the air.

With that, their rematch was on.

◆ I only wanted to be loved

Siesta and Hel's fierce battle had already lasted for more than ten minutes.

When the bramble whips attacked her, Siesta's musket shot them down with perfect precision—and when Hel capitalized on those openings, holding her saber at waist-level and leaping at her, Siesta swung her musket like a sword to counter it. I hung back, attempting to provide cover fire, but—

"Assistant, you're in the way."

"Not fair..."

With the help of her overwhelming experience and instincts, Siesta fought on equal terms—or no, even better—with an ultimate foe who had the land itself on her side.

"—Goodness. You're so desperate, it's ridiculous." Hel had taken a big leap backward to put some distance between them. She was smiling with a frustration that didn't match what she'd just said. "So you want to retake my master that badly, do you?" she sneered, then snorted contemptuously.

More importantly...

"...Your master?"

That phrase tugged at me.

From what Alicia had told us earlier, she'd been created inside Hel's brutal personality. Hel was the dominant one, and Alicia was her shadow. But from what Hel had just said—

"—Are you telling us you took over Alicia's body?"

Had Alicia really been the dominant one, and Hel the shadow? Had Hel forcibly flipped their power dynamic?

"I didn't take it over." Hel narrowed her red eyes. "I switched places for her sake." She insisted that it had been a kindness. "This body is a little different from the other SPES officers, you see. Originally, she was a normal human."

"What...?"

According to what I'd just heard at that lab, the members of SPES were all artificial beings who'd been cloned from Seed's cuttings... No, wait. That was wrong. I knew a pseudohuman *who wasn't like that*.

"Bat..."

The blond guy I'd met at ten thousand meters, three years ago, was a semi-pseudohuman who'd forcibly attached a SPES ability to his own body. Had Hel—had Alicia—originally been human as well, like him?

"However, because of that, they were always performing all sorts of experiments on this body."

Experiments—the word sent goose bumps prickling across my skin.

"She was always crying out from the pain and the heat. It sounds as though my master went through some truly torturous experiences. Then one day, when she finally couldn't take the pain any longer—I was born. My master created me."

...So that's what had happened.

It was a textbook case of dissociative identity disorder. After long-term emotional and physical agony, when she was unable to take it anymore, she'd created a different personality to reduce the psychological damage. Hel was a shadow personality that Alicia had made for herself.

"That is how my master and I are connected. Our suffering halved, our sorrow halved as well. That is how we've lived so far."

"In that case, I'll end both the suffering and the sadness for you right now."

A daydream raced across the battlefield; any further conversation was useless. Siesta launched herself off the ground, closing the distance between herself and the girl in the military uniform so fast, you could barely see her.

Determined and resolute, she pointed her gun at her.

"Oh, I forgot to mention one thing," Hel murmured softly without so much as flinching. "Suffering halved, sorrow halved— And of course, we share pain equally as well."

The next moment, Hel's head abruptly fell forward, and then...

"...What? Where am I?"

She looked around blankly; the cruelty in her eyes nowhere to be seen. And then her eyes landed on—

"Huh? Kimizuka?"

I was a short distance away, and she spotted me first thing, but she didn't notice the other individual right in front of her or the gun turned on her. The muzzle fired a shot.

"Eeeeeeeeeeeeeeeeeek!" With a scream, the girl crumpled to the ground. The bullet seemed to have grazed her; dark red blood streamed from her right shoulder.

"Alicia...!" I shouted.

"Kimi...zuka..."

...! I'd been right. It really was her. Convinced, I tried to run to her, but—

"Don't come over here."

But the one who'd shot Alicia warned me over her shoulder.

"—Siesta, that's Alicia! We can't..."

"I know. That's why I didn't aim at anything vital." Siesta kept the gun trained on Alicia.

"My, my. How kind of you. If you'd shot through her heart or her head, you two would have won."

In the next instant, briars burst up right under Siesta's feet.

"...!"

She instantly withdrew, retreating to stand beside me again. A few meters beyond the riot of brambles, the girl in the military uniform unsteadily got to her feet, holding her shoulder.

"So my master is that important to you."

The red eyes beneath her service cap had reverted to Hel's cold ones. There was no doubt about it: Hel was in charge now, and she switched with Alicia's personality whenever she wanted...!

"However, I won't lose to anyone who's that naïve. This time, I will carry out my mission as SPES."

Hel's red eyes opened wide, and she sprang on us with her sword. At the same time, a horde of brambles attacked us. If we tried to fight, Hel would probably flip back to Alicia. In that case, we wouldn't be able to lay a hand on her—

"Oh, it really was a lie."

Quietly, Siesta murmured.

It sounded a lot like what she'd said to Bat three years ago, on that hijacked airplane. That sentence meant shit was about to get real.

"What are you talking about?" Hel tilted her head, caught by surprise. However, the briars didn't stop moving. They surrounded Siesta and me...and then withered away.

A drop of water trickled down my cheek, and I looked up. "Rain?"

There was a helicopter up there, high in the sky. Was it scattering some sort of liquid...?

"Weed killer," Siesta said. "It's a custom-made, super-fast-acting variety. Don't worry; it has no effect on humans."

"Always ready for anything, huh...?"

It had been a counter for that biological weapon, a technique that killed plants and left humans alive. Ms. Fuubi was probably the one in that helicopter.

"...!"

Hel, still holding her military sword, attacked on her own, while Siesta swung her musket like a blade again.

"What? What about me is a lie?"

However, Hel's hands were trembling slightly around the grip of her saber. In response, Siesta said:

"You have no real interest in SPES, do you."

She spoke without mercy.

"...I've told you over and over. I am obeying fate...and acting in accordance with the will of SPES. That's why I'm—!"

Her red eyes were wavering. For the first time, Hel seemed genuinely off balance—and there was no way Siesta was going to let that opportunity slip past her.

"You said so yourself," Siesta reminded her. Her expression remained steady.

"You are a completely new being, created by Alicia's defensive instincts. Meaning there's no way instincts as a member of SPES could have taken root in you."

...! So that was what this was about... If what Hel had told us earlier was true, the one who'd had SPES abilities and instincts to begin with was Alicia. Hel was only an acquired personality Alicia had created in self-defense. By rights, Hel shouldn't have instincts as SPES.

"That means you're just *a fake* who's been desperately trying to get close to SPES."

Hel was staring at the ground, and Siesta verbally cut right through her.

"Then...," Hel murmured. When she raised her head, her face was suffused with anger. This was the second time I'd seen her this way. "Why would I do that?! What reason do I have to do all this for SPES...?!"

That's right; she'd been just as angry back then, too.

Siesta must already have realized it, in that instant.

Once again, the detective spoke to the girl in the military uniform, as if reasoning with her gently.

"You probably wanted your father to love you."

◆ The monster cries

"—!"

"You just wanted love. You wanted someone to see and accept you. That's all."

"No!"

Hel's pupils had dilated; she adjusted her grip on the hilt of her military sword and raised it high. The blade closed in on Siesta's throat—but Siesta dodged it lightly, and the tip sliced through empty air. Hel's attacks didn't seem as spirited as they had earlier. Siesta's theory had been right on the money.

"Then why are you so upset?"

I fired at Hel's feet to keep her at bay.

"...!" Hel scowled a little, retreating temporarily.

"Let me rephrase that. Why did you switch personalities with Alicia back there?" Siesta asked a second question as she kept her gun trained on Hel. "Because you actually hoped I wouldn't aim at anything vital if you did? ...No. You just wanted to hurt her."

"...Well, I won't deny that. After all, I was born just to take on the pain of the dominant personality. Maybe I had some desire for revenge."

"Yes. Yes, that's right. You have emotions. You aren't a plant...and you're certainly not a monster," Siesta said. "However...you're still lying."

"...Lying..."

"The real reason you're forcing Alicia to take that pain isn't a thirst for revenge. It's jealousy."

"—! Silence!"

Hel flew into a rage. By the time I realized what was happening, she'd leveled her sword and locked blades with Siesta.

"You were jealous of Alicia. She'd caused you all that suffering, and yet she'd found companions in myself and my assistant. You hated her so, so much...and you envied her."

"No... No, no!"

"I'm not wrong. You just wanted to be loved. You wanted friends."

"Silence!" Hel's red eyes glowed.

"You are going to kill yourself, here and now...!"

The next moment, Siesta had drawn her handgun from its holster and set it against her own temple.

Hel had used her ability, that power to interfere with human consciousness and control actions.

However—

"Siesta, you're not going to die."

When I spoke, Siesta promptly released the gun.

"Wh-why...?" Hel stared at us, confused, and Siesta explained.

"It's simple. I trust my assistant more than anyone else—even myself." Siesta glanced at me, then spoke to the ultimate enemy who dominated the field in front of her. "Even if my mind tries to embrace its own death, if he firmly denies it, then I'll believe him without a second thought. That's all it is."

"...! Then..." Hel's eyes turned to me. At that—

"Assistant, you won't die, either," Siesta said to me.

It was the spell that held our odd partnership together.

We both trusted each other more than we trusted ourselves. That was all it was.

Really, that was all.

This one minor thing, unconsciously cultivated over those three years, made us invincible.

And that was the one and only way to cancel out the brainwashing inflicted by those red eyes.

She could say whatever she wanted to try to take control of my mind, but if someone I trusted more spoke to me, I would be free again.

To me, that "someone" was Siesta—and to Siesta, it was me.

If you say that's a deus ex machina development, well, at least call it the power of our bond, all right? It had taken three years to develop, too disgustingly stubborn for us to break even if we wanted to.

"—! A bond? That's just— That's not...!"

She didn't want to admit it, but she couldn't summon the words to deny it, either.

Hel dropped her sword, holding her head. This was probably the plan Siesta had come up with.

If we were going to save Alicia, of course we couldn't kill her body. We'd have to remove Hel's personality—and so Siesta had struck at Hel's psychological contradiction, trying to destabilize her emotionally.

"That's right, Hel. You don't have to obey that sacred text. You don't have to kill anyone else. You can have friends without those things. You'll create bonds, too."

I could see what Siesta was trying to do. "You don't have to force yourself to listen to what that Seed guy says..."

But before I could continue—

"I can't afford to lose." Hel retrieved the red-hilted military sword. When she raised her head, her eyes were blazing red.

"Hel, you're..."

"I admit it." As Hel turned to face Siesta, she wasn't wavering the tiniest bit. "I wanted to be loved. I wanted to be needed. I wanted someone to say that my birth had meaning... But nobody would have done it. It isn't that I wanted companions, no matter who they were. I just wanted Father to love me. I wanted *him* to accept me."

Hel pointed the tip of her blade at Siesta.

"And I'll live, fight, and destroy the world for it. That is my survival instinct."

It was something completely unbreakable, an enormous evil—a conviction.

"That's fine."

The only one who could confront this enemy of the world was the ace detective. With her gun at the ready, Siesta accepted the declaration of war.

"We've killed the plants. We've rendered your red eyes useless. All you have left is that sword. Let's settle this, shall we?"

"Getting cocky because this is gun versus blade?"

"No. It's because this is me versus you."

"You're really irritating."

"No matter how we met, I'm sure we never would have gotten along."

"You've got that right. So let's end it here." Hel lowered her center of gravity, poised to draw her sword.

With lightning speed, she slashed at Siesta—and just then…

"…! An earthquake…?"

Out of nowhere, the ground bulged upward; with a roar, it began to crack. *Did we miss some of the roots?* I wondered, and I'd braced myself, when—

"Assistant! Look out!" Siesta shoved me hard, sending me flying.

The next instant, the ground jolted up dramatically. A large rift opened between me and Siesta—*and something emerged from the ground.*

It looked like a huge reptile, and its grotesque coloring seemed familiar. However, it was much larger than it had been before, a full ten meters long now. As the earth rumbled, it bellowed—and then it spotted its target.

"Siesta…!"

The biological weapon had been revived: Betelgeuse.

Its eyeless head was turned toward Siesta and Hel.

"—Over here, monster…!"

I squeezed the trigger of my Magnum until I was out of bullets…but Betelgeuse didn't seem to care. It faced the others, ribbons of drool trickling from its enormous lower jaw.

"Is it…hungry…?"

Betelgeuse was a monster that ate human hearts.

There were two people on the other side—and a hungry monster was bound to prioritize numbers over anything else.

"Siesta!"

Beyond the huge monster, I caught a glimpse of a girl with pale silver hair. Immediately afterward, there was a howl like a whale's moan—and then a large burst of red like a flower.

In that last instant, my eyes met the girl's, and she seemed to be smiling.

◆ To the most......person in the world

"Bitten by my own hound."

After the dust cleared, what I saw—was Betelgeuse's enormous body. Even after its vicious rampage, it was lying on the ground, with Hel's foot planted on its head.

And—

"Siesta..."

My partner was lying on her back. Red blood was dripping from the left side of her chest.

"They were keeping it isolated in the lab, but maybe the smell of food drew it here," Hel commented, then stabbed her sword into Betelgeuse's neck. The monster seemed to be dead already.

"Oh, *I want you to stay where you are for a bit. Don't move.*"

Her red eyes glowed...and I stopped in my tracks. Before I even knew what I was doing, my feet were trying to run toward Siesta.

"I've lost a little too much blood..."

Keeping me pinned with her ability, Hel walked right in front of me toward Siesta, her steps unsteady. Now that I was paying attention, I saw that the left side of Hel's chest was also deeply wounded, and dark red blood was streaming down her front.

"Now then." Hel reached down toward Siesta.

"...! Don't you touch her!"

I tried to run toward Hel...but my body wouldn't move. It was like I'd turned to stone. If I wanted to undo the brainwashing from those red eyes, someone I trusted from the bottom of my heart had to be there with me. And she was gone.

"My heart's been damaged again, you see. I need to trade it for a new one," Hel murmured.

Of course. In London, as Jack the Devil, she'd stolen heart after heart. It had been trial and error, a search for the one that would be most compatible with her body. Now, since Betelgeuse had attacked her heart and damaged it, she was trying to get a new one again—from Siesta.

"...! Stop! If you want a heart, I'll give you mine! Just not her... Anyone but Siesta!"

"I told you earlier, remember?" Hel briefly stopped moving and glanced at me. "You're going to be my partner one day. That means you have to take care of your life...doesn't it?"

Hel narrowed her red eyes—then plunged her right arm into Siesta's bloodied chest.

"Stop...!"

But my body wouldn't move. I couldn't even blink as I watched the horrible scene play out.

"I'll take the ace detective's heart. Now I'll be unequaled." Hel drew her right hand out of Siesta's lifeless body. A pulsing heart rested on her palm.

"S-Siesta..."

All I could do was stare in a daze. As I watched, Hel reached into the hole in the left side of her own chest, took out her own heart, and casually crushed it in her hand, then pushed Siesta's heart against her chest. The heart slipped into her body, as if that was where it had always belonged.

And it was over.

In just a few motions, Hel had stolen Siesta's heart.

"Finally, I've found a heart good enough for me. Now I'm sure Father will...," Hel murmured with satisfaction. She didn't spare a glance for Siesta's corpse. She just looked at the sky behind her. A white moon was shining there.

"Siesta..."

Numb and drained, I stumbled over the broken ground to Siesta. Hel's work was done; I'd been released. I tripped several times before I finally reached my partner's body.

"Siesta."

Kneeling, I pulled her bloodied corpse into my arms. Her body was small and thin. I didn't have to check her breathing to know she was dead. Her eyes were still open. I closed them with the palm of my hand, then wiped away the blood that had spattered her pale face with my fingers.

"Siesta." I called to her, one more time.

There was no answer. Of course there wasn't.

The detective was already dead.

"......—, ...—!"

I'd thought I wouldn't cry. After all, she hadn't been my lover or my friend. We were only business partners with a common interest. Siesta wasn't special to me at all.

And yet no matter how many times I wiped them away, drops of water kept falling onto her face.

"...I'm sorry."

With a trembling hand, I stroked her head, cradled in the crook of my arm.

As before, Siesta still didn't answer.

"Give it back."

Instead, I spoke to Hel.

Gently laying Siesta's body back down on the ground, I used what strength I had left to stand up.

"Give it back? Give what back?" Hel turned around, apparently mystified.

"That heart belongs to Siesta. You're going to give it back."

"That's out of the question. This is mine now." As Hel spoke, she set her hand over the left side of her chest.

And something inside me snapped. "Don't touch Siesta with that filthy hand!"

The next thing I knew, my feet were moving. Everything in me wanted that thing dead—my body, my bones, my flesh, my blood. I drew my knife and lunged at Hel.

"I don't understand." Knocking my knife aside with the guard of her sword, Hel frowned. "The first time we met, you told me you didn't trust anyone but yourself."

I swung my blade over and over...but before long, Hel gave me a look of disgust and slashed my right arm. The knife fell to the ground. *Okay, then—*, I thought, clenching my left hand into a fist.

"...So it's come to this, then. *Your fist won't reach me.*" Hel's red eyes glowed, and my body froze up again. "But now, you're bleeding out and yet you refuse to relax your fist. As you try to strike me, your bloodshot eyes are even redder than mine. Why?" she asked. "Where is that anger coming from? Is it because of what you mentioned earlier? That bond?" She wasn't finished asking.

"What were you? What were you to her?"

My raised fist wouldn't move. Maybe because of the blood I'd lost, my feet weren't steady, either. Still, I flogged my stalled brain and thought.

What had I been to Siesta?

I didn't need Hel to ask me that. I'd been thinking about it myself, all this time.

How had she seen me?

But it was too late to know now. The dead won't tell you a thing. I didn't know what Siesta had thought of me, and I'd lost all hope of ever finding out.

Still...

I thought with my unsteady brain.

What if I turned the question around?

What had I thought of Siesta?

That day, we'd met in midair at ten thousand meters, and we'd traveled together for the past three years.

...Frankly speaking, I'd been sick of it.

After all the crap I'd been dragged into before, I'd loved ordinary routine more than anybody, and I'd wanted to stay in that tepid bath forever. But she'd dragged me out of there—and that leap out of the window at the cultural festival had ultimately been a leap into the extraordinary.

I don't know how many times I'd prayed to the gods, and to the ace detective, to give me a break.

Listen, do you have any idea how many times I almost died?

How many times did I get injured, or pulled into gunfights, or go for three days without food or water, or camp in bear-infested mountains, or chase murderers, or get kidnapped, or locked up, or fight pseudohumans and biological weapons, and get into unfair situations, and after all of it hear my partner say, "Are you stupid, Kimi?"—

Do you have any idea how many times I smiled?

Siesta acts cool most of the time, but did you know it's actually pretty easy to make her laugh? She doesn't like people seeing her be too genuine, so whenever she feels a laugh coming on, she always turns away from me, takes half a minute to get her face back to normal, and then gives me an

"Are you stupid, Kimi?" I crack up watching her, and Siesta gets cranky, and that's the full routine.

She's more of a kid than you'd think.

It's fine for her to tease other people, but she won't let anyone tease her. She's bad at lying. She's bad at being social, too. She can't wake up in the mornings. She can't even wake up at noon. She sleeps a lot, eats a lot. When I buy two kinds of cake, she gets mad if I try to pick one first. And then she eats them both. And enjoys the hell out of it. Then, when she sees me watching her and laughing because she's completely unbelievable, she takes her fork, scoops off the bit with the strawberry on it, and holds it out to me.

That was what Siesta was like.

You think she was an ace detective who fought the world's enemies?

That wasn't what she really was.

Yeah. I only stayed with Siesta because she was fun.

Yes, I'd had way more than my fill of hardship and pain and bitterness over the past three years.

But in a thousand unfair cases, I'd smiled ten thousand times.

I'd smiled with her.

"Just what kind of relationship did Siesta and I have, you ask? How did I feel about her?"

That's been completely obvious right from the start.

Strength flowed back into me—or maybe it was an adrenaline rush. My bones creaked; my muscles shook; my blood boiled. I didn't really care, though. This might just destroy my body, but it didn't matter. As long as I took out Siesta's enemy, that would be enough.

"You broke the mind control..."

I saw Hel, her red eyes wide.

I raised my left arm, which was wet with blood, and yelled out my feelings for my partner, who would never hear them.

"She's the most precious person in the world to me!"

My clenched fist bore down on Hel; her face was right in front of me.

Just before I made contact—

"I'm incredibly grateful for that love confession, but are you planning to scar up your beloved's face?"

I heard some rather familiar snark.

◆ I'll come to see you, one more time

For a moment, I didn't know where the voice had come from.
"...Huh?"
Hel didn't seem to know, either. She cocked her head, her face expressionless.
This was extremely weird.
The mystery voice I'd just heard had been exactly the same as the voice of the person standing in front of me.
What the hell?
As my mind jammed with question marks, the girl in the military uniform suddenly dropped the saber she'd been holding. Then she stared at the results of her own action in surprise. It was as if, for the past couple of minutes, another will had been controlling her movements and speech.
"What... Hmm? ......This...is..."

Hel's face spasmed.
Then, in the next instant, the color of her right eye changed from red to blue.

"Siesta, is it you?"

The left half of Hel's face was astounded. The other half was watching me steadily.
Now I was sure of it: Siesta was alive, inside Hel!
"No, that... That's—ridiculous..." Hel's red left eye glared at the blue one right beside it. "You won't...get away with this... Taking...over my body...without...permission..."

"Be quiet. I'm talking with him right now." The girl squeezed her eyes shut tightly. When she opened them again, both were blue.

"Siesta, you..."

"I went and made you cry, didn't I?"

There was no mistake. It was her.

She was borrowing the body of Hel, her mortal enemy, but the one speaking to me was Siesta. That fact made my knees go weak, and my eyes grew hot again.

Siesta was still alive.

"Siesta, I'm..."

"Assistant, there's no time, so listen carefully." But Siesta didn't bask in the joy of our reunion. She just kept on talking to me. "The thing is, my heart is *rather special*. For example, by moving my own consciousness into it, I'm able to hold on to my sense of self inside someone else's body."

"That's..."

Was it similar to the phenomenon of memory transference? There had been cases all over the world of organ transplant recipients inheriting the memories and preferences of their donors.

Since Hel had stolen Siesta's heart, Siesta's memories and awareness had also been partially transplanted into Hel. That was how Siesta was borrowing her body to speak—

"I came up with several different plans, but it really would have been difficult to defeat Hel in the truest sense of the word."

"...! Siesta, are you saying you—?!"

"Yes, this was the only way. *I had to infiltrate Hel and repress her mind.* That was the only way to oppose her."

...! Meaning that back then, Siesta had intentionally... She'd known she was going to die!

That wasn't— That was just ludicrous!

"I told you, didn't I? A real ace detective resolves the incident before it occurs. I'd known for a long time that things would turn out like this."

"No... That's not fair... All along, you..."

So she'd been able to see our destination right from the start?

In that case, why... Why?

"Because if I'd told you, you would have stopped me." Siesta, wearing Hel's form, gave a rather lonely smile. "I have a favor to ask you, Kimi."

"...No way."

"Listen."

"No."

"Are you stupid, Kimi? This is no time to be stubborn and you know it," she said, putting out a hand and stroking my head. "I'll infiltrate this body and keep Hel's vicious personality in check. If I do, Alicia's personality should wake up again."

"...! She will?!"

"Yes. After all, this body has Cerberus's ability... You understand what that means, don't you?"

...Ah, I get it. The three heads of Hades' guard dog. She was saying this body could house up to three people. Alicia and Hel had already been there, and now Siesta had joined them.

"She may have lost her memory again, but I want you to ask for her help—and someday, I want you to defeat SPES."

That had been Siesta's true secret plan.

The one and only stratagem to defeat Hel and let Alicia live.

"—! But then what happens to you? If Alicia's personality wakes up, then yours will disappear along with Hel, right?! Don't you dare... I won't let you!"

Sacrifice Siesta to save Alicia? If that was the solution, I didn't want it!

It didn't matter what form she took. We could even be enemies.

As long as you, your mind, is still alive somewhere, that's enough for me. So I won't let you do anything this selfish!

"I thought you'd say that." Siesta gave another ghost of a smile. "It's going to be all right, though. Alicia has things I don't. I'm sure you'll be able to get along well with her. Remember those two weeks," she told me gently.

"—I told you, don't act like this is decided! I haven't agreed to..."

Just then, the ground rocked under my feet.

Had I lost too much blood? No, that wasn't it... I smelled something sweet.

In one buoyant moment, a euphoric and fuzzy feeling swept over my mind. Through dimming eyes, I saw that an enormous flower had bloomed from the corpse of the biological weapon.

It was pollen.

The sweet-smelling powder drifted to us on the wind.

"...Maybe this is fate as well. It's been three years since then." Siesta gave a troubled smile.

Three years... Oh. The Miss Hanako incident at the cultural festival, three years ago. This pollen was the drug that had rampaged through my middle school.

"So it came from a flower from this thing's body, huh...?"

I knew what these conditions meant, even though I desperately didn't want to.

"No... I don't want to...forget..."

The very first side effect of ingesting this pollen was memory trouble. Inhaling this much of it had to carry a substantial risk. I might forget these three years entirely, and all about Siesta, everything—

"It's all right."

Maybe Hel's body had an immunity to the pollen; Siesta was still standing firm. As I swayed, she let me lean on her shoulder.

"Well, you may forget a little. What happened here, for example, or the things I've told you. Still." She smiled. "You won't forget me. You won't abandon your mission. You'll sigh and whine that it's not fair, and you'll keep working with Alicia for me."

"That's...not okay... I won't..."

By that point I couldn't even stand, and I sank down right where I was. Black was creeping in at the corners of my vision, and it was getting harder to hear.

"I'm...your assistant... I won't...be...anybody else's...partner..."

"...Ha-ha. That's a nice thing to hear, here at the end."

I was sitting down. Putting a hand on my shoulder, she smiled softly at me.

Was this another side effect of the pollen? Was I hallucinating? Hel was our mortal enemy, but right now, I could only see the partner I'd spent three years with.

"I don't...want to forget... You'll... I'll...always..."

"I'm telling you, it's all right. Remember what I said? This whole time, we've trusted each other more than we trust ourselves."

"...So, I should...believe...what you say?"

"Exactly. Have I ever been wrong?"

...No, she hadn't. Not once.

You were always right. Way too right.

Every once in a while—I wanted you to be wrong.

But my throat wouldn't let those words out.

"The next time you wake up, I'm sure I won't be there anymore, but..."

Live. And thrive.

Was it my imagination? Siesta looked like she was crying.

She wouldn't cry, though.

Was it because she was in a different body?

With large tears trickling down her cheeks, Siesta grabbed my shoulders and shouted.

"Listen to me!

I won't forget you, Kimi!

Even if a ruthless enemy hijacks my mind, even if I forget everything else, I'll remember you!

It may take a while!

A week, maybe!

Or a month!

Or a year!

It may take a long time!

Even so, I promise—!

This body will come to see you, one more time!

I swear, I swear it will!"

After I heard all that, I slumped over onto the ground.

In the last glimpse I caught of Siesta, she was smiling through her tears.

Side Siesta

I didn't have much time left before my consciousness faded out completely.

I decided to spend it with my sleeping assistant's head on my knees, stroking his hair. He was sleeping like a child, with tear tracks on his cheeks.

"Are you stupid, Kimi?"

When I poked at his cheek, my index finger met with a springy resistance. Honestly, right now, he was more like a baby than a child.

"...That's why I intended to say good-bye on the boat."

Because my assistant would cry. Because he'd cry for me.

To be honest, I hadn't meant to let him see me at the end. I'd meant for us to part for the last time on the way to the island... And yet he'd chased me all the way out here. Hadn't Charlie yelled at him?

I swear—

"Kimi, I suspect you like me far too much."

I'd made that joke before.

I parted his bangs with the ball of my thumb. *Why does his face look so cute when he's asleep?* An anger I didn't really understand welled up in me, and I laughed a little.

"I'm sorry."

I knew he couldn't hear me.

"I'm sorry I ended up dying first."

But I had to say it.

"Actually, there's one more reason I went with this reckless plan."

It was during that party you held for me in London, to celebrate my recovery. Do you remember what Alicia said? She said she wanted to go to school someday.

And so I decided to grant that wish.

"I could have just defeated her. Killing her would have been easy. But then…Alicia said that."

She wanted to live. She wanted to go to school.

I'd risked my life for that…and by tasting defeat, I'd won. This way, when Alicia wakes up in this body, I'll be able to send her to school.

Huh? Why would I go that far, you ask? Well, I mean—

"Because a detective's job is to protect the client's interests."

I knew what my assistant would have asked if he'd been awake, so I answered him.

"The thing is, it looks like that may take a little time."

If I was going to make it so that Alicia could go to school or lead a normal life, I'd have to stabilize her mind first. Even if it was a different personality that had done the killing, the knowledge that people had died at her hands might be too much for her.

I'd have to do some internal work and memory correction first, and also create a new identity for her. I'd already put that red-headed policewoman in charge of that. Right now, she was probably on her way to provide Charlie with backup, but it wouldn't be long before she came to retrieve me and my assistant.

"I've asked her to lie to you, too, but don't be mad at her, all right?"

Specifically, she's supposed to tell you that I defeated Hel and temporarily neutralized the threat of SPES, and that Alicia is safe and has been sent to live in a distant country. Otherwise, you know you'll do something silly like try to take SPES on by yourself.

So, until all the preparations are in place… Even if it's just for a little while, I want you to go back to your daily routine.

I want you to live those average, uneventful, peaceful days you longed for.

"I'm sorry for yanking you around so much over these past three years." I stroked my assistant's head again, and again, and again. *I'm sure this is the last time this will happen.*

"I fought with you constantly, didn't I?"

As I thought back, what came to mind was Kimi's profile as he muttered, "Not fair."

Had I really been that unfair? Had I given him nothing but trouble? I'd gotten carried away a minute ago and said I suspected he liked me far too much, but had that been completely untrue? ...The idea made me a little nervous.

"Still, I had fun, at least."

If I said that, would you laugh? Or maybe you'd get mad and tell me not to break character... Well, this is the last time, so let me have this, all right?

The apple pie I ate with you tasted sweeter than when I ate it alone.

When we lived together in that cheap apartment, it felt almost as if we were a couple, didn't it?

The casino was fun, too... Oh, but I'm pretty sure you lost your shirt there.

Come to think of it, every now and then, you still gaze at that photo of me in the wedding dress, don't you?

A few days ago, we drank alcohol for what was probably the first and last time. That did not end well...

What time should we wake up tomorrow? What should we eat, and where should we go? Will we get a request for a new job? Finding a lost cat or something would be nice and easy. Oh, right: I spotted some good teacups at a shop I walked past a little while ago. I'll buy them next time, so let's brew some fancy tea and drink it together. Don't worry, there'll be enough time for a cuppa. And then the day after tomorrow, and a week after that, and a month after that—

"I wanted to drink tea with you a month from now, too."

I wanted to see your profile as you said "Not fair" and sighed.

And your smile... I don't think I could ever have seen enough of your smile.

"I didn't...want to die."

But my job is to protect. And I'll protect you.

That is my mission. After all, an ace detective is someone who protects the client's interests.

I promised back then, remember? I said I'd protect you. No matter what kind of trouble finds you, I said I'd protect you with my life.

So relax and sleep, just like you're doing now. Stay in your dream; sleep in that way I might have thought was a little bit cute. It's all right. I'm sure someday, someone will wake you up.

And I know she'll hold you close, *in my place.*

"I never did give this to you, did I? I'm sorry."

Finally, I took out the red ribbon—which I'd stealthily slipped into Hel's military uniform during that last fight—and tied it around my head. *I wonder if she'll still be wearing this a year from now.*

"...That's right. I'll have to think of a name, too."

That would be the final spell that kept Hel's consciousness sealed.

"Hel— The name of a cold queen said to have ruled a country of ice."

Her new name should be warmer, at least. Something to melt others' hearts.

A name that suited that smile of Alicia's, as dazzling as the summer sun...

"Listen, Assistant."

I called to him, one last time.

"Remember this. The name of the one who'll wake you up someday is—Nagisa. Nagisa Natsunagi."